The Crystal Mask

No part of this publication may be reproduced, distributed, or transmitted in any form or by any means, including photocopying, recording, or other electronic or mechanical methods, without the prior written permission of the publisher, except in the case of brief quotations embodied in critical reviews and certain other noncommercial uses permitted by copyright law.

The story, all names, characters, and incidents portrayed in this production are fictitious. No identification with actual persons (living or deceased), places, buildings, and products is intended or should be inferred.

Originally published on April 25, 2024

The Crystal Mask

The Mardi Town Series

Zineb Bizriken

To the people who associate with the fullness of the moon and its darkness

Chapter I

"It is confirmed. The property in Groove street is yours for the second weekend of February, including Friday night. I hope your stay is delightful," I said as I waited for them to end the call. This last call was my fifth. At last, I can let loose and erase that tight smile I'd been maintaining—despite having been on the phone. The smile was necessary to bring my voice a pitch higher. My cheeks are left stiff all across. The ache will fade away over time.

The call was from yet another couple.

They were booking a romantic get-away because aren't they all when Valentine's day is so near. Money entered my pockets and I can only be happy, but the words my girlfriend and I were hoping to book the property on Groove street tickled my brain to death. Don't ask me why.

I miss the free-minded travellers, businessmen in town for a convention, or the people simply in need of a break. Those are my usual customers. In February, there seem to be no business conventions and buy one get one free promotions.

It won't be long until nausea is no longer a daily occurrence. The time frame's a few business days after Valentine's Day. People who are busy during Valentine's week often celebrate it a week later. You're not safe until the whole ordeal is truly over.

I'm holding on to my coat, given that February's breeze is harsh and cold. You would expect that an expensive designer coat would include the bare minimum: buttons. It's apparently more fashionable to leave the coat open or clutch the fabric, helplessly.

I pulled my hair tie down, in hopes my hair keeps my neck and the edges of my face warm. Did it make a difference? Not really. I hate the cold as much as I hate most things. However, when living in the heart of Mardi Town, walking is a more practical option. Everything's at walking distance. Spending money to avoid walking in the cold for mere minutes would be a waste.

I walked while taking a few calls and already, I was near my destination. The tourism office where my best friend Auburn works. As a self-employed person, I do as I please. And I choose to eat lunch with her each day. It's even written in my schedule—it would be if I had one. This allotted time allows me to vent about everything that irked me this morning. This time is well needed.

I left my coat on the golden coat hanger at the entrance and was welcomed by the receptionist.

"Hello, Mrs. Mint," she said with a smile I quickly discern as fake. It seems she's not fond of seeing me here every day. I don't see why. I've asked nothing of her. Then again, she doesn't appear passionate about her job either. All she does is watch the clock, eager for it to reach five. Who could blame her?

I returned the smile to be polite, but it held no meaning.

I rushed to the first office on the left and blurted: "Auburn, I'm bursting with words."

"I'm not your therapist, Rene," she replied, a teasing smile on her face.

"You're my best friend. If you're not listening, who will? Besides, you can complain too. It's a win-win situation."

"There's nothing to say. My life isn't as fun as yours," she said as she curled a strand of red hair with a pencil. "I'm stuck in this office typing away things that don't interest me."

"Life can be fun if you chase your dreams."

I sat down in front of her dark wooden desk. Due to limited space, her office only accommodates a desk and two chairs—one for herself and another for a guest. At least she had privacy. I enhanced that privacy by closing the door.

"It's not that easy," she always said.

It's ironic for me to talk about dreams. The career I'm pursuing has never been my dream. My dream is what comes with it: a continuous flow of money. And it never was easy.

"I brought bagels for lunch. Freshly made in late street," I say, swinging the paper bag back and forth near my cheek.

"Thank you. I was starving," she said as I gave her a salmon cream cheese bagel and a napkin. "Your bribe worked. Tell me your complaint of the day."

I crossed my leg over the other and leaned back.

"Love."

"Again?" A sigh left her mouth before the bagel reached it. "For someone who hates love, you mention it all the time."

"I only mention it because they reminded me of it. Do you know how many calls I'm getting from couples booking properties? I wanna throw up. Am I missing something? What's so great about love?"

"Hey, no mention of vomiting at lunch time. And you know all about love. You felt it before, didn't you? Love is butterflies. It's warmth and tenderness, it's—" I had to cut her off.

"Love is a lie. It's a pretext."

"One unpleasant experience and you became the Grinch."

Unpleasant is downplaying it.

"I didn't steal Christmas."

"No, you stole Valentine's Day. That's the sequel. I'll have to give them a call to say their heroine is right here in Mardi Town."

"I didn't steal it. Yet. But jokes on you, weren't you the one who was crying for an hour on my bathroom floor last week because you got dumped?"

"He wasn't the right guy," she said.

Last week's memory must already be

fading in her mind.

And another mention of the *right guy*. I'm starting to think he's a myth. A legend. He's like Santa Claus for adults. His only purpose is to bring a sense of comfort at this point. My other best friend, Laine, was also present last week; she brought ice cream and told Auburn: "He wasn't the right one. The right guy will come when it's right."

"Anything aside from your hatred for love?" she said, her bagel nearly finished.

"There might be something. Something that is positive."

"Finally," she said, slamming her back against the chair.

Dramatic much.

"I've done some thinking about how to improve my business and eventually bring it to the next level."

Just thinking about it brings in the butterflies. This is my kind of love.

"You're already rich, your business is doing well and you're looking for more?"

"I haven't reached my limit yet, if there

even are limits."

"Of course you haven't."

Was that sarcasm?

I can't even call myself a millionaire yet—though I'm not far from it. Of course, I want to keep climbing. It's tempting to be satisfied with my monthly earnings, but why not aim higher and unlock my full potential? I must take this step, It's crucial.

"I'm thinking of buying a house."

My business comprises renting out apartments for a short period of time. I myself rent those properties. Prior to signing a lease contract, I ask the owners for permission. I tell them ahead of time about my business. Some refuse and some accept. I approach them as CEO of the Mint Company, along with a business plan, rather than adding two lines to the initial email. Through this business, I can earn at least 65 thousand a month. While it's enough for daily life, the fact that part of the profits are spent on rent bothers me. It's money I'll never get back.

"This could be better. It'll also be less

stressful," Auburn said.

"Much less!"

Renting out a property comes with a mountain of risks and limitations. Not all customers are polite and mindful. If they do damage, the blame is on me. And I receive a strike. Even if I repair it—and I have to—it remains an incident to be noted. These strikes stress the heck out of me. I'm very fortunate to never have had a contract terminated. Alas, it very well might happen someday. With a house of my own, I'd have fewer worries and a higher income. Less stress, more money—what deal could be sweeter?

"And you saved up enough for it?" she asked me.

I tried to hide my face behind the paper bag. The sight of a bank account brimming with zeros—before the comma—blurs the stop signs. Or it's that you're going so fast you can't see any.

"For the house I want, I don't think I have enough."

"Don't tell me it costs a million dollars?"

"Auburn, you're a mind reader now? How'd you guess the exact amount?"

In her widened eyes, I can see the words lunatic written.

"Why go for such an expensive house?"

"Well, buying a property is a long-term decision. I'd rather go big at once. And I have the means for it. Can you imagine how much I'll earn from that property? I won't need the others anymore. It's hard to manage multiple properties that aren't even yours, you know?"

"I don't how it feels to earn 65k a month," she said, wiping the corners of her mouth with a napkin. "How are you gonna buy it if you haven't saved up the one million?"

I was glad she asked.

"Easy, I'll take out a loan."

"A loan for one million?" she said, her chin down to her neck. "Your credit score must be to die for," she scoffed.

"To be more precise, I'll ask for a mortgage. I'll have to give them a 20% down payment, which is around 200k and I will receive 800k. The monthly fees will be quite high, but they'll pay themselves with the business."

My speech now over, I give her my proud smile, the one where the corners of my lips reach my cheekbones. I am bursting with excitement for this.

"You have it all planned out, huh? Don't forget to invite me to the housewarming. I'll bring my worthless tray of homemade brownies."

"I love your brownies. Their worth can't be determined because of how good they are. They're incomparable."

She tapped the back of my hand. "That's sweet, but let me work now. Lunch break's over."

"That soon? Time is flying today."

"You're the one who's flying, Rene."

I'm not sure why, but that last comment didn't sit well.

Chapter 2

I found myself at Java Haze on Late Street, ordering another cup of coffee. I couldn't resist it. This street is called late Street because you're so at ease here that being on time turns nearly impossible. This fun fact might not be a fact at all. Consider it a believable silly legend.

If you step foot in Late Street, you'll feel yourself forgetting about the rest of the day. This street is full of peaceful establishments, such as coffee shops and bookstores. No one in a hurry stops by a bookstore. They take a good look around, find some books that pique their interests and ask themselves, "I have plenty of unread books sitting on my shelves. Should I really get this one? Should I not?" I include myself in this statement. Remember what I said about the blurred stop signs? Bookstores were definitely on a crossroad somewhere. Initially, I didn't even consider whether or not to buy a book. If I can afford it—and of course I could—I'd buy it. That was a mistake. Success blinded me. Digits in my account too.

Going back to Mardi Town, if it's fun you're looking for, then you'd have to visit Groove Street. There, you can find the hottest dance clubs and even better, late night jazz clubs. During the day, you'll see me holding a cup of coffee in Late Street and at night, you'll see me with a glass of whisky on Groove Street.

"A cigarette with that?" The waiter and owner of Java Haze asked me.

"Robert, you know I quit."

This is the last coffee shop in town that allows smoking indoors and thus sells cigarettes on the side. Hence the name Java

Haze.

If requested, you can receive a cigarette with your coffee, placed on an ashtray. Java Haze is heaven for smokers and hell for those who quit. I experienced a lot of stress at the beginning of my journey here. It's a shame I resorted to smoking to cope. I quit once I realized the effect was so temporary it created additional problems. Cigarettes solved nothing. The success of my business now allows me time for self-care. And part of self-care is a healthier lifestyle. I still frequent the café because I'd gotten close with Robert. Aside from the cigarettes, Java Haze still is a hell of a pleasant place.

"Just testing you," he said before walking away, his dress shoes leaving a trail of clicks.

This coffee shop is my unofficial workplace. I can clock in daily and rent costs as much as a cup of coffee.

Hands on my laptop, I scrolled through house listings. Out of the few fancy houses Mardi Town possesses, not many have a million dollar price tag. They're either lower or higher. Once I become richer, I'll sweep off the market. I'll make them all mine and won't blink at the price tag. I read no get-rich-fast book nor will I ever write one. I don't wake up at 5 in the morning to drink my freshly brewed coffee and gaze out the window to catch the sunrise. I have time for these activities, yes, but they're not of my preference. Life is to be enjoyed in one's particular ways. Slowly, I am introducing you to my ways. One of them is being the hard-working Rene Mint, CEO of Mint. Co.

Unless you have a winning ticket, becoming rich is never easy. I tested my luck and in no time; I realized you needed to work hard to even believe in luck.

Let's keep on with the hustle then.

The house that had supernatural rumours, capable of drawing all the curious travelers, was recently sold. I'd buried the heart I'd given it and searched for a better house. It's crucial to have a specific property in mind before requesting the loan. And this is without doubt the fun part. Ah, to look at pictures of rooms designed for perfect pictures and to visit those houses.

In the process of scrolling, I'd let my espresso turn cold. The already bitter drink gained a darker edge. They say to drink coffee freshly made, whilst I find hot coffee that turned cold more charming. The bitterness feels like a slap on the tongue. I'm no masochist, but the taste is fine.

"Too much screen time is bad for your eyes," Robert said, walking towards me. "I'm sure you quit smoking for your lungs, so don't neglect your eyes."

"I've only been here for 30 minutes," I remarked.

"Switch to paper," he said, plopping down a newspaper on my table. "Here's today's paper. You'll find listings there too."

"No one cares for me the way you do. Thanks."

Robert shoved his hands in the pockets

of his apron and opened his mouth, only to close it. He gave a nod and returned to his counter. He's not very expressive and gets flustered when receiving compliments.

Robert is a middle-aged man who's clocked in nearly every day in this café since the age of fifteen. He saw me through my best and worst. Java Haze is the first place I visited when coming to Mardi Town. I booked my accommodation in advance, but had to wait a few hours before clocking in. The first coffee shop I'd laid my eyes on was Java Haze. I was exhausted, hurt from recent happenings, and nervous about this journey I took on. I ordered a coffee and Robert surprised me with a warm coffee cake on the side. I can still remember what he'd said then.

"Welcome to Mardi Town."

Once I heard that, I was confident in my decision. I knew I'd found my home.

I unfolded the newspaper and hesitated to jump to the real estate listings. The headline of the front page was too attention grabbing.

A crystal-leaving Robin Hood in Mardi Town!

Colour me intrigued. I flipped it open to read the relating article.

One person has been identified as the mastermind behind the recent robberies in Mardi Town. The odd character steals valuable items like jewellery, cash, expensive artwork, and small antiques. They leave behind a counterfeit crystal by the front door. Many think the crystal is a trademark.

Here in Mardi Town News, we are calling him Robin Hood. Upon investigation, it became apparent that the robberies were limited to wealthy households. The nickname Robin Hood of Mardi Town was given to him because some believe he distributed the stolen money to those in need. Charity organizations have reported a growing number of donations, all made under anonymous pseudonyms. Because the amount given is always an odd number, not matching the exact amount stolen from a house, it is impossible for the police force to prove which donated money is stolen money. They are working hard to locate the thief despite the lack of traces. Investigators are facing difficulty in this investigation due to the lack of fingerprints or footprints on site.

Already, the public has mixed reactions. Some call the crystal-leaving Robin Hood a hero, while some prefer the term criminal. We are open to receiving opinion texts concerning the crystal-leaving Robin Hood.

Send them to:
MTN
1140 Midnight Street
Mardi Town
or
submissions@mtn.com

The news to me is insane. Nothing of

this scale ever happened here in warm and welcoming Mardi Town. This article left me with mixed feelings.

"Did you read this before handing it to me?" I say, walking to the counter. "What's your opinion on this Robin Hood?"

"I think you should make sure to always lock your doors," he replied, his eyes stern.

"You too."

Robert started as a waiter until he became the owner of this establishment. And he earns a lot from the coffee and the cigarettes—it's a hit! He's been loyal to the original owner, more than his own blood. When he passed away due to old age, his lawyer announced Robert would receive ownership of the shop. I heard it was quite the scene when the family heard about the news. I wish I could've seen it, or at least have been there for him. The family's return to claim the business after their father's death had caused numerous disturbances to Robert's fresh start.

"I have nothing expensive in my house; I'll be fine," he said, his eyes softer.

Robert never splurged on anything other than coffee equipment. He takes such good care of his equipment that he doesn't need to splurge that often either. I'm not sure he even has the time to spend his money. I rarely see him out of the shop. He devotes his life to work. Java Haze is his life. I wonder where the money he earns goes to. Maybe he's planning to have a luxurious retirement, assuming he decides to retire.

***

When I returned to my apartment, I slipped into a hunter green silk robe. I set a vinyl of my icon, Lana Del Rey, on the LP player and opened a store-bought Tiramisu. I allowed myself to rest on the armchair facing the tall windows. Though I can't bring myself to wake up early enough for the sunrise, I can bring myself to savour the sunset. Living in Mardi Town gives you the perk to see colourful lights every night. Every edifice I can see holds its own colour, either from the roof or its sides. Garlands are a must here. The festivities never end so much that no one remembers when they started. By the end of the day, just sitting in a cozy armchair with a good book and dessert allows me to unwind.

My favourite spot for alone time is here. I drown in my thoughts and let the music take over. I'm not particularly sentimental, or so I believe. Most of my thoughts are insignificant ones. Or you could simply say that I don't take myself seriously.

This store-bought Tiramisu falls short of the one I enjoyed in Italy. That's also another place I blew my money on. I visited Italy just recently. Initially, I asked my friends to tag along, but they thought it was too expensive. I offered to pay for their tickets. They refused and took offence. I understand where they were coming from and I wish they understood me as well. It wasn't to flaunt my wealth that I offered, but because I wanted my friends with me on that trip. Once I went, they found it mean for me to still go and every day for a week when I returned; they reminded me of it. For all one knows, If I hadn't gone, they'd say I was making them look bad for not letting me go. No answer was ever the right one. Not even for a split second did I ever fully trust my own decisions. Each step of the way, I remain troubled with doubts. You could go as far as calling it borderline anxiety. No one sees it though. The only thing they see is the confidence of a self-made rich woman, just as I desire. They'll keep seeing this crafted image for as long as I can keep it up.

Chapter 3

"Bap bap birou bap bap," the Jazz singer sang.

From the stage, Primo, the saxophone player, sent a wink in my direction, along with a greeting nod. As if he came from a 30s movie, he wore a brown suit and tie with his fedora hat hanging on the ear of his chair.

I diverted my eyes to the beignet covered with powdered sugar on my table. It's best not to engage with this character. He smiles too much and his eyes are playful. It often feels suspicious. You'd think he had something up his sleeve and was waiting for a signal to jump right in. I've never given him a signal and I'm not planning to. Then again, some men interpret everything as a signal. One look and I've supposedly fallen for their charm. Pathetic.

More importantly, this place is another café I frequent—only once in a while. I come here solely for the live Jazz that happens on Thursdays. The coffee's sour and the beignets, too sweet. I could never be a regular here. Let's say that apart from the coffee and sweets, at least the place is pleasant.

Voices in the café interacted softly in order to not muffle out the singer's voice. Decorative leaves on the walls trembled from the warm air coming from the vents. Dainty light bulbs formed a line on the ceiling, projecting small amounts of warm yellow light. And at the table across, a little girl stared at the stage with glimmering eyes and a mouth open. A dream had bloomed in her little heart. Rina, the singer on stage, excels in her craft. Her voice embodies the genre that is Jazz. That voice belongs to an old soul; everyone says it. She chases away the fatigue and lights a flame in our hearts.

"My baby's gone. He's left me." She sang, swaying her hips left to right, flaunting the gemstones dangling off her silver dress.

She stood on the stage barefoot; it's a quirk of hers. Her neatly cut bob of blond hair reached her chin.

"I only have to believe it." She ended the song on a low note and removed her gloved hands from the mic stand.

The room filled with applause overpowered the noise of espresso machines. A smile on her face as she told us she'd take a slight break. She waltzed to the edge of the stage where her black cone heels stood. With her shoes on, she walks toward me, flashing the gummiest of smiles. On stage, she gives off a cold and chic image and once offstage, her bright persona comes to life. Her age—nineteen—is more reflected in conversations rather than in performances.

"What's the vibe today?" she asked, taking a seat.

"Vibes are decent. Yours?"

She took off her black gloves and made eye contact with a waiter to request a coffee.

"My vibes are immaculate!" her head rested on the palm of her hands, like a flower. "I love Thursdays. I can sing for the fun of it with no pressure."

Rina spends her days cooped up in the studio with her producer Lance. They are both perfectionists and workaholics. They make an exception to their rules for Jazzy Thursday in Memoire café.

"Rene, I don't know if you've noticed, but there's a guy who's been checking you out all morning. I saw him from the stage."

I scoffed.

She continued, "Take a subtle glance. He's the one wearing khaki pants."

"I won't move an inch. You know I'm not interested."

"One way or another, someone will open

your heart again. The right one will."

My trigger words.

"Someone is already opening my heart," I told her, my fingers resting on my chin.

"Really? Who?" she said, leaning forward to grab my arm.

"His name is..." I spoke at snail pace to raise her expectations. "None other than money!"

"I can't believe you!" she tapped my arm before pulling back, a frown forming on her face.

"You only have to believe," I sang, mimicking her voice.

Rina brings the silly out of me.

"You're never going to change, are you?"

"Not a chance."

Love is and will always be overrated. I'll repeat it for as long as they mention it. It's a waste of time, emotions, and money. Even flings aren't worth it anymore. Sure, love sounds nice—coffee dates, midnight motorcycle rides, secretly kissing in the library... If it doesn't end like Romeo and

Juliet, it'll find another way to end. Love cannot escape the cycle of beginnings and endings. That's Amore!

"No events lined up for me?" Rina asked, bringing me back to my senses.

Rina is a work contact of mine and I come here on Thursdays to support her and propose her events—when I am planning one that requires a singer. I consider her the best voice to represent Mardi Town. To show outsiders the Jazz of our town.

To bring in traction to town and eventually my business, I collaborate with Mardi Town's tourism office—the MTTO. I give ideas for events and I aid with the planning. I'm not paid for the work, but money enters my pocket from the tourists needing accommodations for these events. In exchange for my services, I'm allowed to advertise my apartments in the event brochures and posters. It's a win for all of us except for hotels. Well, what can I say; the world is changing. The competition could motivate them to improve.

"Some events are in the works, but I

need confirmation. For that reason, I can't tell you anything yet."

"You're working hard," she said, taking the cup of coffee to her mouth.

"Always. You work harder, though."

She let out a sigh and drifted her attention to the cup's handle.

"I've been in a rut lately. I'm lacking inspiration, and so is Lance. Why do we always experience it simultaneously?"

"Another proof you're soulmates."

Rina and Lance are childhood friends turned lovers. That I envy. There's trust and comfort in those kinds of relationships.

"Are you sure you're not interested in love?"

I hesitate to answer this time. Fear lurks behind my disinterest. The hurt had been too massive. How can I trust someone again? I'm human. I do crave love and affection. I try to ignore it, thinking it'd be wiser to do so.

My eyes don't curve when I send her this smile and I say, "I'm sure, and I should probably go now."

"Already?"

"I have an important meeting to prepare for; I really have to go." As I stood up, I readjusted my chair and added one last thing, "You can have my beignet if you want, and have fun for the rest of your Jazzy Thursday." I ordered the beignet but its appearance reminded me of why I usually don't order it. "Inspiration will come your way."

She smiled, her hands already on the beignet—her tooth's sweeter than mine.

A wave of the hand and I'm off, the fabric of my open coat dangling with every step. Out of pure curiosity, I made sure to catch a glimpse of the gentleman whose attention I supposedly caught. A smirk rested on his face as if he'd won the game. A pitiful little thing is what he is. I suppose I fulfilled his boredom with this misunderstanding I'll never clear up.

***

Today's boots are Miel's. A classic. At least that's what I've been told. Does it show that I'm new money? There used to be days where I didn't dare glance a second longer at price tags with over two digits. Now, I don't dare to look away. If you had the money, wouldn't you?

I'm even acting like new money, wearing my sunglasses in winter; the sun isn't even in view. And I'm wearing a coat supposedly expensive enough to protect me from the cold. I ought to buy a warmer coat, regardless of its aesthetic. Upon further reflection, it's February. Spring's around the corner. I can take a month of cold. I'll just walk faster.

As I told Rina, work awaits me. My meeting at the bank for the loan is tomorrow and my meeting to visit the house is today. After spending the night flipping through a real estate magazine, the perfect house presented itself. I did look for it, but I'd like to believe it found me. I'd also like to imagine the money I need is already in my pockets. There is no reason for the loan to be declined. I have more than enough proof to show that I can repay it. Knowing all is going according to plan, I RSVP'd to the open house.

This oh-so-desirable house has many fine aspects to it. From afar, I can recognise its burnt orange walls and hunter green balcony rails. The house is tall—almost like a building—and is perfectly situated in the centre of town. Each room has a balcony and bathroom of its own—that would earn me extra points.

After handing out the RSVP slip I printed out in a hurry this morning, I was admitted inside. Amazement in my mind as I see how wide and spotless the place is. The floors are slick and woody. At the entrance, there's a long oriental rug underneath a wooden table. On that table rest three flower vases all evenly spaced out. The white vases are adorned with hand-painted blue lines. And the flowers inside are a mix of magnolias and marigolds. I would've looked at them the entire visit but then the staircase caught my eye. The glorious spiral of the flight of stairs is a feast to the eyes. As if they were made of the finest wood and the cleverest hands, the steps didn't creak. I can only hear the clacking sound of my heels. I slid my hands on the railway—for the fun of it—until my eyes faced the chandelier that rested at the top.

The dripping crystals sparkled away with some help from incoming sun rays. The numerous windows make it so the house is well illuminated during the day. I went upstairs to see the rooms first. When entering the first room, I knew what to expect, having seen pictures in the magazine. Yet, I continue to be impressed. Each room has its own distinct charm. One has a bed stuck to the window with clear curtains blanketing the front and back. Another has a single wall plastered in tawny brown wallpaper and golden round frames. The room next door has a bathtub unlike the other rooms, which have showers. This feature gives me the right to increase the price of this bedroom. Adjacent to it is a room comprising a walk-in closet with enough space to accommodate one more person—who knows, perhaps I could turn it into a budget room. The last room has an alcove where one could lodge in a desk and declare it a home office.

Soon I'll see no use of the properties I am renting. I'll have a house that brings just as much profit—even higher when I'll pay off the mortgage.

When I returned downstairs, I felt the love no man could ever give me. A few steps from the entrance, a library stood in front of my eyes. A multitude of shelves filled with books of all sizes and colours. And in each corner, an armchair for a peaceful reading session. For a second there, I might have wanted this house for myself. If I could live in such a place, managing multiple properties won't be trouble, a roaming voice in my head said. Of course, I wiped the thought away. But I didn't fail to compromise with it—it's the only way I got rid of it. When I earn enough money to buy a second one million dollar house, then I'll claim this one and use the other for business.

The common room houses a sturdy wooden piano. Enchanted by the grandiosity of the piano, I sat by it on its matching bench. My mind was blank at the sight. I've never played the instrument, nor have I touched a key before. Controlled by my intrusive thoughts, I reached a finger out.

"The piano can stay if you'd like." Her voice startled me into abruptly pressing a key; a quick note filled the air.

When I followed the voice, I saw a lady with black hair, straight like needles and a folder thick with papers. She must be the real estate agent, I immediately thought.

"The homeowners want to get rid of it unless a buyer would like to keep it. They'll pay for the fee for its removal if it's unwanted," she said.

"No. It's perfectly fine to leave it," I said, feeling myself drawn to the piano. If someone hears us, they'll think I've already bought the house.

I can only imagine having a guest that enjoys the piano. They'll bring entertainment and joy to the other guests. This house will be filled with laughter and smiles.

With a nod, the agent brought me to a place I hadn't had the pleasure of discovering yet. And as expected, the kitchen is also immaculate. The space is wide and well lit. The counters are marbled. There are plenty of cabinets. And there is a large window for ventilation; perfect for when the heat of cooking is unbearable, when they accidentally burn a dish, or simply for a gust of wind on a feel-good day.

I turned to the agent; with pleading eyes. I told her, "I'll formally give you an offer tomorrow. A slight detail is preventing me from making an offer today. Is there a way you could wait?"

"We have received a few offers already and we'll accept more until the end of the open house—which is Saturday. You have until then," she replied.

Hearing that offers have been made is making me nervous. My overly-confident self would like to back out. Then again, all is not lost until the very end. For me, the end and perhaps the beginning will be tomorrow. If all goes well.

Chapter 4

I am biting my bare nails. I've never gone to a nail salon for the simple reason that I would ruin their delicate work whenever my anxiety kicked in. My body shook from the inside, forming an earthquake only I could sense. And my legs are wrapped on those of the cold metal chair. Even without the presence of my coat, the heat is prevalent. The needle of the clock inched closer towards eleven— which is the time of my meeting.

I don't know why I'm stressing. Where did my confidence go? Where is the woman who claimed to have the money in her pocket? I remind myself of the fact that whoever's waiting for me in that office will be wide eyed when they see my yearly revenue. If they've done their research prior to the meeting, the contract might have already been drawn and the meeting will be more of a congratulatory party.

I plopped my feet on the ground, brought my hands to my knees and lifted my chest, sitting straight. A conscious breath and I managed to gain back the composure of Rene Mint, for I knew my name would be called.

"Miss Rene Mint? Mr. Malt is ready to see you."

Malt? As in the malt in my Friday night whisky? While I have quit smoking, drinking is still a work in progress. At the very least, I've decreased my intake—so much that I haven't passed out in months.

Up on my feet, I made my way to the door and twisted the handle, the touch of it chilly. The nerves of earlier were a simple fluke. Mere habits of the past making an unwelcome appearance. I'm okay. From the start, I knew not to doubt the outcome of this project. And so, with renewed confidence, I marched in.

"Pleased to meet you, Miss Mint," the man on the office chair said then. "I'm Avel Malt." With grace, he lifted his arm and, with a gloved hand, pointed to the seat across his desk.

To wear gloves indoors is a bit odd, yet fitting for a citizen of Mardi Town. The tendency to be old-fashion runs in their blood. That is one of the reasons I'd decided on coming here.

Apart from the gloves, he dressed modernly. He embodies the business casual look with an oversized wheat coloured suit. He skipped the tie and left the jacket open, showing a white shirt that seems breathable.

"The pleasure is all mine," I replied.

In front of me sat the man I'd needed to convince. Mr. Avel Malt, a seemingly young banker—somewhere along the twenties, I suspect. He looked at me without a smile and somehow I enjoyed it. He has no interest in me or my case. I can tell. This appointment is one of many. If he were overly enthusiastic, I'd see through the facade.

"How may I help you today?" he asked, his brown eyes cold as hail and his tone sharp as a fishing hook.

What an interesting character.

"I'm here for a loan," I said.

"I trust you brought the appropriate documents."

The fishing hook isn't only sharp, it hooks. There's something enticing about his rigidness. I am not scared of his tone, only amused.

"Of course I have," I said before bringing the folder in my bag to his range of reach.

The folder has tax slips, revenue reports, etc...

He flipped through the pages without a word or even a nod.

"What is the purpose of this request?" he said, his eyes on the pages.

"I'd like to buy a house for my business.

I'd like to have more control over this work and owning a house, I believe, is the best way," I said, assuming he already knew of my business and the question was a formality. I kept it short and sweet since we both don't seem to have time to waste.

"I've done my research on you, Miss Mint, and am aware of your affair."

That's it. I nailed it already. If he did his research, then he must be impressed by my journey and the wealth I've amassed at such a young age.

"How much would you be hoping for?"

Now we're getting somewhere.

"A million," I said right away, showing no sign of irresolution. Then I took out another folder, "I've already found the house in question as you—"

"Let me stop you right there, Miss Mint," he said, placing a hand on the folder that was halfway there. "I am afraid that I cannot approve your loan."

I must've heard wrong.

My fists clenched underneath the table and I said: "I don't see why you couldn't. I did my research too. I am able to provide the 20% down payment and pay the bill every month.”

He had the audacity to cut my words short and disapprove of my loan. On what basis?

In spite of my—justified—denial, I kept at it.

“You’ve seen my profits. I reckon they’re higher than your salary.”

There’s the mistake. Speaking rashly can often lead to childishness, for the mind of a child is underdeveloped.

Before I could attempt to retract that last statement, he started to laugh, his eyes creasing in an almond shape. His laugh was short and mocking—anyone could see that. His laugh made me regret thinking I’d wanted to retract my not-so-polite words.

“Your profits may be high at the moment, yet I can’t help but think they’ll drop in the near future.”

“Why do you think so?” I questioned, keeping my calm like the adult I hope I am.

“Your business is relatively new and, at

first glance, doesn't seem stable. It could suddenly drop and lead you into bankruptcy."

This man is a sworn pessimist and if he thinks he can bring along my business to his black hole... Well, he's in over his head.

"How would you know, Mr. Malt? My business is doing fine. No, it's doing better than fine. The numbers climb month after month; I've yet to hit rock bottom."

He intertwined his hands, his arms on those of his chair.

"You've said it yourself, not yet," he retorted.

This is not happening. In my head, the loan was pre-approved. I came here to celebrate and this ridiculous man is telling me that my business is bound to fail. He'll not see the end of it, and neither will I.

"I contest your reasoning," I said, inching closer to the desk. "You have no proof to back your so-called theory."

He set his hands free from his grasp and flaunted the back of his hands to the air.

"It's not a theory, Ms. Mint. I've been in

this line of work long enough to know giving a large loan to a person of your age with little experience is a risky move."

Been in this line of work long enough, my ass. He merely looks a few years older than I.

I'm not a fan of violence, but the option's tempting. He's so calm, it's insulting. Only his lips moved on his face. The remaining features were set in stone. You could imagine how cold it feels to speak to such a person. You'd feel merrier talking to a wall.

And he had to keep at it. "Do you have any other inquiry?" he asked, seemingly unfazed.

I scoffed, my insides boiling.

Yes, *I'd also like to withdraw my money from this bank* is what I wanted to say, but, "This isn't over, Avel Malt," is what I said instead.

He had the gall to look away and hide a snicker with his hand. What triggered him? The fact that I declared war or the fact I used his full name? I'd love to repeat myself with more spite and wipe that small but noticeable snicker off his face.

***

"You're redder than a hot chili pepper, Rene," Robert told me as he laid down the triple espresso I asked for.

I knew my choice of coffee would be throwing oil to the fire, even so, I went ahead with it. Feelings are things I don't suppress anymore. The past taught me that indulging in my feelings is better for the heart.

"That jerk refused my loan."

That jerk stepped over my dreams with his polished dress shoes, and I can't help being aggravated by it. Who can blame me?

"What's your plan now?" Robert was calm in contrast.

He's probably lived through a fair share of ups and downs, so much that he can glide through them now. He settled down. Little poses difficulty to him at this age and state. I envied his stability. I'm still a youngster running with a blazing fire under my feet.

"What's there to plan? How can I improve when I don't see the problem he pointed? There's no fault; what's there to fix?"

The issue he mentioned is nowhere to be seen. How can you answer a question that was never asked? How do you find a solution for a non-existent problem?

"Perhaps, wait it out. If you go back a year later with proof that the business is still thriving, he'll have no choice but to accept."

His answer's rational, as expected.

"A year? A year's too long for me to wait. The house I picked is counting on me for this Saturday."

Though his solution is wise, I don't want to admit it is a solution.

"There will be plenty of houses for sale next year," he said.

The word patience was thrown out of my dictionary a year ago. That concept is no longer understood by my source of consciousness or even my subconscious.

"Sorry, Robert. Young people are known for living in the moment and being reckless. I have an image to uphold," I gave him a crooked grin as I spoke sarcasm-filled words.

"You do you," he said before returning to his counter as a few customers arrived. When he said it, his tone was warm as the flame of a candle. I'm sure he meant it as: Continue to be yourself.

I will.

For the time being, I'm sitting at Java Haze in complete disbelief. I am without a plan. I never considered a Plan B because I was confident it wouldn't be necessary. The scene I replayed in my head included a smiling banker telling me there would be no problem. I vividly pictured my hand inserting the golden key into the door of my dream house. I've even gone as far as picturing myself shopping for vintage-looking furniture while my wallet wept silent tears. The frequencies I sent out must have clashed with Mr. Malt's overly negative frequencies.

Would it be an exaggeration to say I'm going through the five stages of grief with denial and anger coming through simultaneously? Is it denial If I truly believe I can do something about this? The remaining stages—bargaining, depression, and acceptance—will retreat and let me be on my way. In the absence of loss, there is no grief.

From now on, I won't be apologetic for what I've said to him nor will I apologize for what I'll do in the near future. I reject his rejection.

Chapter 5

With denial renting every space in my mind, I marched back to the bank—thinking I've simply met the wrong banker. Bad luck lead me to that eccentric banker, that's for sure. While there may be one bank in town, there are plenty of bankers. Ones who'll use numbers and logic as reasoning instead of cynical intuition. With that in mind, I asked to see another banker at the front desk. Problem is, upon hearing that I spoke with Mr. Malt, each turned their head away. With a cough and an excuse, they brought me to their door. His name was a trigger. When hearing it, none bothered to lay a hand on my file. For the next meetings, I learned to not mention his name and pretend this meeting was my first—regarding the loan. However, when entering my name in the system, their faces froze briefly before escorting me out. I assume his name was somewhere in my digital file. I figured he either warned all the bankers or that his name enough was fearful to them. I suppose the reason is the latter. If their trust for his judgment was the reason they'd refused me, fear wouldn't have shown on their face. One blinked more than once to make sure he'd read his name right. One turned so stiff I thought she'd turned to stone. Another ceased to speak and began communicating in hand motions.

After the long hour spent at the bank, I acknowledged this new reality. Avel Malt is the only person able to approve my loan.

And so, we're moving on to the second stage of grief, anger. My fist itched to be thrown to the wall. In my head, it pierced through every wall until it arrived at Mr.

Malt's office. He then trembled with fear. My head—being in a different dimension—also saw him on his knees, sweat dripping from his forehead as he signed the loan approval.

"I'll sign it. Please don't hurt me," he said.

If only.

I stormed off the bank, my coat in my hands. My wrath kept me so warm, I'd suffocate with an extra layer on. My insides burned while I contemplated how I could safely release this rage. Dealing with anger has never been my strong suit. I'd let it burn for as long as it could. But that was the past. When I came to Mardi Town, my mind went through rebirth. All has changed about me. The past will never make a return.

Given my current state, I should be spitting fire all around.

***

"You don't look well," Auburn told me, catching a glance before sticking her eyes back to her computer screen.

Time to speak with the best friend in her office. Don't we all complain to our friends when something doesn't go our ways?

"My loan was rejected," I said in a whimper.

The more I said it, the more it became a fact. Well, it is and I've moved past the denial... Or at least I thought so.

"That's strange," she said, removing her hands from the keyboard. "Even after they saw your profits?"

I was grinding my teeth, "Yes. That guy dared to say my business didn't look stable. My business is thriving!" I threw my hands up and dropped them on my thighs, making a deafening sound.

"Maybe he was right?"

...

Maybe he was right? Did I hear this right?

Flustered by her comment, I couldn't help but ask, "And what do you mean by that?"

"Life is all about ups and downs. It's not normal for a business to only experience ups. Rising so quickly could foreshadow a rapid descent."

She didn't dare to look in my eyes as she talked. She brought her focus back to the screen and fidgeted with the mouse.

"I had those ups and downs. Sure, the numbers don't reflect them and that's because I worked hard. You saw everything and you..."

Auburn knows of the hardships I went through. She listened to countless of my rants about rude customers, delayed service, trashed rooms and plenty of problems that nearly broke me and put my work in peril.

Ever since the day she'd told me I was the one flying, I found her different. As if a strange idea formed in her head and she was changing for the worst. Of course, I shouldn't be rash when thinking of my best friend. I was sure it was nothing, yet here she was planting that idea in my head again. The supportive friend I knew of is no longer. I thought by now she'd notice and rectify herself. I thought.

"I was talking about the numbers. They're the ones that had no ups and downs," she added, her voice smaller.

Maybe her words were meant to be taken lightly, and that she didn't mean harm. Words that sound hurtful at first can be realistic ones and caring. Auburn's love might be evolving into tough love. For all I know, my rage could have clouded my judgment.

***

I can no longer dwell in my anger and do nothing about it. This fact alone nearly made me go straight to the depression stage, but I can't possibly defy the order. Instead, I'll walk in the line of the game board and position myself on the third space, bargaining. And right at the source. Based on my experience at the bank, I doubt they'll allow me to see him or anyone else. I could go, for another matter. The bank wouldn't go as far as blacklisting me. I'm a pretty big client of theirs. The numbers in my account speak on my behalf. They could only go as far as refusing my loan. Refusing a rich client's loan is going far, though. If I give in, they'll think themselves able to push the line further. You can mark my words. I won't let myself get to the last stage—acceptance—as I'll never accept this and experience grief. There's no grief in the absence of loss—remember that. This reality will turn into a dream of the past and my dream of owning a house will turn into my current reality.

Auburn had started to get busy, and I had to move past the lull anger. What better place to gather my thoughts and form a strategy than Java Haze?

Striding in, I immediately got a whiff of tobacco. The scent is hard to resist. My nose needed a distraction and I could only think of coffee. The closer I was to the oak-counter, the safer I felt. You see, Robert was grinding coffee beans. It's a wonder that the smell of cigarettes was stronger. I understood why upon turning right. A group of old men were smoking, creating a cloud of smoke hovering over their heads. A person who's never smoked would be disgusted while the one who's quit smoking is full of envy. Robert, won't you ask me for a cigarette on the side? This time I'll consider it. I gazed at them for a while until Robert snapped me back to my reality.

"You'll have to drink at the counter today," he said. "All the tables are filled."

"Really? Well that's surprising," I first said. "Ah, but not that much. You do have a great place." I added.

He nodded as he filled paper bags with fresh ground coffee. He sold packs of them on the side. There's a reason for his wealth —side businesses—and the patience to handle them.

I scanned the coffee shop to make sure Robert hadn't missed a free table, but indeed, no table was without a person. My eyes were stunned when they laid on the last table. Because there sat the ridiculous man who stepped on my dream. He played a round of solitaire, like the loner he looks to be.

"Robert, that man playing cards over there. Did he ever come here before?"

I asked, since I've never even noticed him in town before the appointment. He sat with ease. Must not be his first time at Java Haze.

"Avel?" he said, taking a peek. "He's a regular."

My eyes and mind were stunned. I'm more than a regular. I'm mistaken for the owner's daughter. How I never noticed him is beyond me.

His hand rested on his head while his forehead creased with wrinkles as if the game was giving him a tough time. I just wanna ruffle the cards on his table and make him start again. Can't I do that? He drove me back to square one first. I sprung off my feet, thinking of the stage of anger I'm going through. Fate was the one to bring us here. Upon reflection, it seemed more like a curse.

"I'm sitting there," I pointed to Robert.

Focused solely on my target, I disregarded Robert's reaction.

Smoothing my black pants, I settled into a seat at his table. With only two chairs available, we had to sit facing each other. A shame.

"I'm sorry. There's a lack of free tables today," I said, unable to hide my smile.

"The counter is clear," he replied, his gaze still on the cards.

"I find backless chairs uncomfortable."

Adjusting his blouse collar, he sighed and glanced upwards. His eyes were empty and his chin slightly raised.

"You again?"

"Yes, mind if I sit now?"

He didn't answer and probably didn't need to since I'd already sat. I guess he chose to ignore me and go back to his solitary round of solitaire. That I can't allow. My hands went for the cards. In the end, I didn't scatter them and simply spread my fingers all over to obscure his view.

"How about a round of rummy?" I proposed.

His jaw briefly clenched seeing my hands over his cards, but after hearing my proposition, his lips alone smiled.

"I have time to spare," he said, surprising me.

Silence took over while he busily gathered the cards and shuffled them in his hands.

His answer was so prompt it pissed me off. Why couldn't he have done that for the loan? This moment feels like accidentally blowing your only wish on something stupid.

In the midst, the click clacks of Robert's dress shoes approached.

"Two espressos for Avel and Rene," he said, placing the cups in their respective places.

I stared at Robert, whose face neared a snicker. Why did we both have to fancy the same coffee?

"Thank you," I said in a voice smaller than usual.

Avel didn't a show a reaction to the ordeal. I have a feeling nothing much interests him. One would comment on how uncommon it is for young people to drink espressos. Instead, he began handing out the cards. That brought me to the reality of my suggestion. I didn't ask him to play out of boredom—granting I do love this game. It's an opportunity for conversation and bargaining. We'll naturally flow back to the topic of my loan. Perhaps the shock I'd received in his office impaired my capacities and prevented me from adequately bargaining. Now, I'm in my element. My workplace. And I'm with an espresso. How could my anger get the best of me?

I picked up all my cards and started to organize my hand. I wonder if I need to worry about his rummy skills, as I already have to worry about what to say. Who knew I'd meet him here? In all truth, my thoughts aren't gathered. This meeting might be too early. I might've jumped too fast on the opportunity, forgetting that I'm not prepared. Everything I say will be spontaneous, and all I can do is trust myself and hope we can compromise, at least to some extent.

Given that he distributed the cards, he threw the up card—the five of diamonds. I picked up the card, needing it for a set of fives. In return, I tossed my useless king of hearts. Avel—if I can call him that—continued with the poker face. At this point, this is his default expression.

Already I find it hard to throw a line along with a card. That to me is odd behaviour on my part. I spoke well with people barely known to me and with Avel, my head's blank. He emits some kind of energy I'd never come across. His energy is so foreign, it keeps me on my toes and keeps me hesitating.

He took his sweet time to decide whether to pick up my card or one from the deck.

"Won't your coffee get cold?" I said, noticing the steam of his coffee drifting away.

Again, he hadn't looked when he answered, "Mind your own coffee."

Scrunching my nose, I refused to sip my espresso—for my pride.

Never have I heard of this line. Mind your own coffee, huh? Makes me want to use it someday.

Shouldn't I say something back? If I stay quiet after this, I'll look like an obedient scaredy-cat. But when you don't have a comeback in mind, you'll end up saying something idiotic—making the matter worst. I just kept playing. I picked up a card from the deck only to be disappointed. The three of clubs doesn't help my hand.

The game went on for aeons. The rummy is a mix of luck and strategy. A beginner with basic knowledge could very well win against a seasoned player if they receive good cards. You could say it's a game of probability. That's why guessing the level of a player is never easy. It's difficult to tell after the first game, but maybe after a few more you'll know. I don't think I'll go as far as playing many games with Mr. Loan Denier.

"Do take your time picking a card," he told me, the fragrance of his sarcasm invading our bubble.

For a slight moment, I had zoned out and forgot about the reason I sat at his table. I couldn't help but focus on the game. It's been ages since I played rummy. My friends preferred chatting—I like that too. But this game fills you with nerves. Your mind is restless. You're in distress, longing for that last card you need to fold. You pick up card after card only to throw them away. Whenever you see the other player pick up a card, you fear it's game over.

We exchanged intense eye contact, as if we knew we both needed that last card to declare victory. My right foot pressed deeper into the floor; I'm on the edge of my seat—literally. Our poker faces were ruined. His elbows pressed against the arm of his chair. I only need the nine of spade! He too must have a single card missing to his set. His already whole eyebrows appeared fuller when furrowed together. The last card is always the most frustrating of the bunch. As I took a card from the deck, feeling it was the one, a formidable gust of wind blasted its way into the café, taking along our cards. All eyes were fixated on the spiraling dozen of cards. For a moment, the world stood still to witness the sight. I was in awe, my jaw dropping to mop the floor. Lines on his forehead, Avel turned to the culprit—a man whose crime was to open the door and invite the unwelcomed wind. And as the cards dropped to the floor, everything reverted to normal. People returned to their conversations, and I returned to a world without tension. With the cards scattered, my dire need for the nine of spades disappeared. My hand was no longer mine.

I bent to pick up the cards soiled by snow and dirt residues from winter boots. With a sigh, Avel also bent down, picking them up much quicker than I.

"Do throw them out for me," he said, plopping the pile on the table.

"What about our game?"

"Sadly, we'll never get to know the winner," he said, the corners of his lips creeping upwards.

He downed his espresso before leaving, a hand near the back of his head, waving carelessly, much like I do. Weird. Though not the weirdest thing. I had a chance, and I blew it. Too engrossed by the game, I didn't mention the loan. Not even once. What am I to be distracted by cards? Five?

"What was that about?" I heard Robert say, holding a tray on his way.

"My last straw."

Robert's posture loosened when he sat in Avel's place. He rubbed his chin and motioned for me to sit back down. And I did. I couldn't help but stare at the pile of soiled cards. I really blew it.

"How do you know Avel?" he asked me.

"He's the guy who refused my loan."

His body jerked like an exclamation point as everything clicked.

"I guess you tried to talk to him about the loan and judging by your expression, it didn't go well?"

I nodded, bringing my hand to my head. I was this close to ripping my hair out until I reminded myself of how much money I paid to care for my hair.

"You said he's a regular. When does he usually come?"

I'll never give up. Mark my words.

"Every day at 2 and leaves after about 20 minutes. I guess that's his coffee break."

"W-w-wait, you're telling me he's been here every day. Since when?"

Was I blind and never noticed it? Was everything an illusion until today?

"I don't know. Since a long time?"

"Way to be specific, Robert."

"Do I have to remember the first visit of every customer?"

"I suppose not," I said, and we laughed

it off.

"Well, Robert, expect to see me an increasing amount of times."

I stood, inserting one by one my arms in my coat.

He scoffed. "How much more could I see you? People are starting to think you're my daughter."

"Some people even think I'm a runaway princess from a foreign country and I hired you to be my body guard and that there's a secret passage in the back leading to my hideout. Just in case the royal guards come looking for me."

He smiled, knowing how some people here are suspicious of me. I did emerge out of the blue and made a name for myself in little to no time.

"See ya," I said.

I didn't forget to throw out the cards on my way out. At least they were the cheap kind you'd find in a corner store.

Chapter 6

The real estate agent was on the phone and I didn't know what to tell her. The deal with Avel isn't actually done, nor is it near completion. You could compare it to a piece of frozen piece of meat that is bloody and has yet to touch a hot pan.

I couldn't ask for more time now, could I? If I don't have an offer at the end of that extra time, the market will block list me.

"Are you still here?" she asked, her voice hinting impatience.

"Yes, yes. I'm sorry," the first thing I did was apologize.

"Several offers were made, but the

owners are waiting for a more satisfying offer. Now's your chance," she said.

Now's my chance to wave the white flag, you mean. The house is officially out of reach, even if Avel agreed on the loan. These people are expecting an offer exceeding a million dollars. The value has gone up according to the property's popularity. I can't compete with those whose one million came from pocket and not a loan.

"*I-*" am truly embarrassed to back off. At the same time, I understand it must be done. It's pointless to drag it out. And...This could have been an email!

"*It looks like I won't be able to make an offer. I must apologize. Life happens and doesn't always follow the plan.*"

Done, there's nothing more to say.

"*It's a shame, really. Though I understand. Don't we all know that about life?*" She replied.

The call had ended soon after a few more apologies from my part and understandings from the agent's.

I found it hard to imagine my sluggish body getting up from bed. My brain gave multiple commands, but the will was so weak it'd turned phantom-like when reaching my already tired legs. I'd danced too much last night. All energy was gone. Even a night's sleep wasn't enough to recuperate. I had an impromptu clubbing night yesterday. That happens when I feel my body trapping in too much stagnant energy. This energy becomes stress at the speed of light. Therefore, I slid my way to the dance floor and danced the night away. I got lost in an organized chaos: music blasting at full volume, colourful lights flashing from all directions and people dancing like there's no tomorrow. Intoxicated by the music, I was in a transcendent state. Without a care in the world, I danced. I even saw someone looking as crazy as me. His energy rivalled mine. He was drunk without a glass in his hand. He drowned in the ambience. His peculiar appearance had also caught my attention. His hair was bleached ivory. He wore a white blouse along with black belt-like suspenders. Chains propped around the pockets of his leather pants. It's not common to see this style at the club. I was captivated and felt a sense of connection with that person. I wonder if he thought the same of me because I too was not there to socialize; lost in a world of my creation.

Despite a night of escaping, morning returned. And that phone call was enough to blast me back into reality. The house I thought of as perfect will fall into another's hands. Let's not fall into old ways. Let's remain positive. That house wasn't my only option. It wasn't my first choice either. When the one that initially caught my eye was sold, I didn't give up on my project and actively searched for a new house. I'll keep at it until I succeed and won't let myself experience the remaining stages of grief. I'll get a loan and the finest house out there.

And so I get back on my feet—quite literally. As I do, another motivation to leave my room comes to mind. Strawberry cake. My freezer contains a few treasures; items bought on a whim for the day I'll crave it. My past self, cares for me the best.

***

For the sake of indulging in sadness for one last time, I chose to pass by the dream house—the one that stays true to its name. Dreams that come true are no longer a fantasy, but a reality. Following this visit, I'll move on. I'll focus on securing the loan since finding a house is a piece of cake compared to it. I peer at the dark green railings and imagine that I'm staring at myself who is on that balcony. By now, that successful woman would be taking a breather from all the decorating she'd done. With a coffee in her hand, she'd be wondering if the sofa's getting delivered today. What could have been will still be. Onto Plan B, no no, Plan Z. In hopes it'll be the last, I call it Plan Z. That plan's first step is to "coincidentally" meet Avel. His coffee break must have already ended earlier. I can only meet him by the bank. Therefore, I must stroll the surroundings of the bank until he gets off work and finds me *passing by*. The deal will be sealed on that third meeting. They do say third time's the charm.

Alike me, the sky seems to be in production. The sky is covered in white with nothing else in sight. That means snow will fall at any given minute. The blank canvas that is our sky appears wider than usual. So much I feel it could swallow us whole. Soon enough, snow began to fall. With my eyes, I followed the first snowflakes until they landed on a pair of black dress shoes. Those shoes turned still in front of me, as though the snow affected them. Curious, I looked up. His hands clenched and his eyes narrowed when they fell on mine.

"What a coincidence?" I told him with a smile.

"I have a feeling it isn't," Avel said, hitting the spot.

Under the bright sky, his eyes appeared emptier. They resembled glass. Staring into his eyes is dispiriting.

"Do you believe in fate?" I then asked.

"No."

He wasted no time to answer.

"How odd to see you here?" I continued playing the role. "I walk by this road every day, yet I've never noticed you. Today, though, I recognized you from the lot."

"Is that so?" he said, with a tone so flat you'd think it a statement rather than a question.

"Are you going home?"

There was a long pause before he responded with his curt answer: "Yes."

I wasn't doing well, seeing that boredom was written on his forehead in bold font. He had just finished work and wanted to return home, I suppose. Chatting is the last thing he'd want to do. After meeting him twice, I know he's never up for chatting. And that at any given time. He's a man who speaks little and cares even less. That's all you'd need to pick up on him.

"Do you ever do things after work?" I asked.

He averted his gaze briefly, only to return it with annoyance.

"No."

I sense a lie.

"What if you did? Would you be up for a drink?"

This is the base of my plan. Alcohol. Once in the system, alcohol brings out mellowness and affects judgment. Perhaps a night at the bar could soften his stone heart. The more friendly we are, the more he'll be open to understanding my business and its glory.

"And why should I?" he ended up answering.

Any man in Mardi Town would have accepted my offer in a heartbeat. Heck, they'd ask me first.

"Why wouldn't you?"

"Answering with a question leads to bad habits," he said.

"We're alike then."

He'd done the same merely a few seconds ago. But somehow, I'm glad he's insulted himself along. The small curve of his lip hinted he might have realized it.

My next line should be something such as *just say yes or no and let us go on with our day.* Alas, that would only shorten the convo. He's not a person I can afford to push away. Both my pride and my ego are bruised.

"It doesn't really matter," he then said, hiding any evidence that he ever was amused.

His face didn't show annoyance anymore. His features eased into emptiness. Like a glass figure crafted without emotions in a bulk-making-factory.

Fog came out of his mouth when he sighed. And his feet are still stuck on the pavement, his posture not budging. My posture is chaotic in contrast. My feet are restless from stagnation. My shoulders are arching forward and my neck is killing me. Let's not forget the weather. If you remain immobile in the cold, you're bound to freeze. All I'd like is to walk some place warm. There's no better place than a bar, right? Alcohol will take no time to warm us.

"I'll be honest," I said. "From the beginning, I wanted to talk about the loan."

"Are you sure it's the only thing?" he said, his empty eyes spiralling with doubt.

"Should there be something else?"

"Usually there is more. Especially when talking with women."

We are far more alike than I thought. The confidence is overflowing. I'm seeing that I might have appeared condescending to a few people I talked to—not that I should worry too much. I had my reasons.

Tapping the ground with my right foot, I answered: "Are you ever going to answer my question?" This man is so aggravating he gets on my nerves. "Tell me Avel, are you coming or not?"

"Were we on a first name basis?" he said, an eyebrow raised.

Enough with the questions!

"If you're stretching the conversation to this extent, you're probably considering that drink. Am I wrong?" I remark, my teeth clenched.

He would've left a while ago if he had zero interest in me.

"You misinterpreted my behaviour. I merely had time to kill. Time to lead on the rich girl."

He passed by me, leaving my body frigid and my mind burning with hell fire. He thought he led me on? Rich girl? I am rich, but why did it sound like an insult? Insults are the majority of what he says. That's why. It's as though he insinuated I'm wealthy because of daddy's money and I skip around town shopping all day long. In reality, my parents owe me money and not the other way around. I never bothered to retrieve that money, having buried my past.

Going back to the leading on part. He's the one with the wrong idea. I approached him for the loan and the loan only.

Nothing about him attracts me. Nothing at all. His hollow eyes seem to impair his vision.

I let him go. I won't think to hold him back. To call his name. To tug on his coat and ask him to reconsider. Screw the fact that I need his approval. Screw the fact that business won't be easier. Screw him and the snow that's falling in acceleration. My lashes are filled with snowflakes, making it harder to see.

I walk back to my apartment, a feeling I'd kept under the radar for so long resurfacing. It's all too familiar. Like history repeating itself. The past was never meant to let you go. The past is a ghost holding to heart the mission of haunting you till the end.

Back at home, the first thing I did was to grab the yellow rotary phone near the front door and speed dial my best friend Lane. She was the one to offer me this phone for my birthday, thus, the number on speed dial could be no other.

The ringing of the phone brought me

comfort, knowing I'd hear her voice at the end of it. Laine is the unofficial therapist of our knit tight group. She chose to call herself unofficial since she doesn't have her license yet. Laine is studying towards obtaining that license and the term of official therapist.

I'd restrained myself from calling her for days because I know how busy a college student is. I didn't want to bother her with a rant that could last hours. I itched to tell her everything, knowing her reaction would differ from Auburn's. There is also one thing about Laine. She knows about my past. My childhood. My teenage years. Every little detail. I'd never planned on muttering a word about it. I buried the hatchet along with the body for there to be no evidence. Yet, I was powerless in front of her. I let her hypnotize me into spilling my story. And as the good friend she is, Laine hasn't talked about it further.

"Rene?" the excitement in her voice broke me.

Chapter 7

After hearing her voice, I lost the ability to speak. I wasn't able to tell her someone's on the line. But Laine is intuitive.

"You should have called before," she said, her soft voice wrapping around my shoulders like a blanket.

With ease, I slid down and leaned against the wall for support. I never considered setting a chair by the rotary phone that obviously can't go far. This phone was merely for aesthetic purposes, yet here I was drawn to it.

"I'm sure you have a lot to say. Spill it,

Rene," she said.

I couldn't find it in me to speak.

She continued. "I won't call you names, nor will I be quick to judge. It's your turn to speak and mine to listen."

That's Laine. She leaves me no other choice when all she says makes sense. I can't think of a way out and there's no more reason to. That's Laine for you. Our soon to be official therapist.

"The past. I feel it coming back inside of me. Not like a déjà vu, but a déjà felt." And that's me having to pause because the words aren't spilling out.

And here comes Laine to the rescue: "Objects can be left behind. Feelings are different. They resurface when triggered. What happened?"

Those feelings for me are poison. No, they're a virus. They contaminated every thought and took over. The wheel is in the hands of virus-like feelings.

"A glass of whisky and I'll be fine," I tell her, at last.

"What therapist or friend would I be if I

agreed to the idea of drowning out your feelings with alcohol?"

"A very understanding one?" I answer, my voice the smallest it has ever been.

I can imagine the frown on her face and the premature wrinkles I perhaps am creating.

On the entire road back home, I imagined myself babbling on and on about how rude Avel is and how unfair this is. My mind was racing. Now, I guess it cooled down. Or I'm repressing by habit. My head was crowded and I suppose the thoughts trampled one another until none could make it to the exit.

Laine didn't press further. She might be thinking I'll confide in her sooner or later. And that she'd might as well give up since her powers are limited over the phone. Eye contact and body language are crucial to analyze and break through one's mask.

"At the very least, don't drink that glass straight. Add some ice and don't chug it," she said, before releasing a sigh. "There are other ways to cope. This isn't it, Rene."

"I don't do promises I can't keep," I say to lighten up the mood.

"Rene!" she shouts.

"I'm kidding. You wanna listen to me putting ice cubes in the glass? But wait a minute, I can't bring the phone to the kitchen; the line's too short."

"Good night, Rene."

"Good night."

She hung up, and for a minute longer, I lingered by the phone, hearing the echo of the dial tone.

Then I made myself a glass of whisky—with ice, as promised. And with that glass, I ponder about my fears. I may not seem like it, but I am a woman of many fears. I live in constant fear that the world I perfectly crafted will crumble down, leaving me in ruins. Tonight I fear that the past will send a wave to bring me back. Unless I ride the wave, I'm bound to be taken away.

***

My eyes are closed and I'm laying down, yet I am in deep thoughts. A glass of whisky isn't enough to make me pass out, now is it? How would it be possible for me to fall into a deep sleep when my head's in a spiral? I couldn't, hence, I didn't.

When I opened my eyes, they automatically went towards the clock on my bedside table. There, the numbers 3:33 flashed in bright red. That means I must have dozed off without realizing it. And what awoke me was the trouble in my mind. Sleep isn't my forte. Either I take hours to fall asleep or my sleep is divided into multiple parts. Every waking moment is an intermission. I don't need that many bathroom breaks.

I tuck myself deeper into the blanket, hoping sleep will find me anew. Intermissions aren't supposed to be long. But then I heard a sound. A sound that rang once. Might have been a bird hitting a window. A dish in the sink slipping down from the accumulated weight. The sound had the potential to be anything; even a trick played by my brain or a lingering sound from a dream I don't recall having. Or so I thought.

The noise came again, clearer, louder, and more distinctive.

Faint rustling.

My ears are sensitive, you see. More than the normal person. That can get annoying. In this moment too, I'm bothered by my sensitivity. I froze, not wanting to make a crinkling noise myself with the heavy blanket.

The rustling continued at a slow pace. With that, I'm sure there is someone in my apartment. It can only be a person since the only animal capable of making its way to the 11th floor by a window is a bird and then there would be flapping, not rustling. Someone is in my home. I am sure of it. What else would rustle for so long? I can pretend to be asleep and check the damage when the coast is clear. When I hear the click of the front door and nothing else after. But what if the damage is so big that it becomes irreversible? I've handpicked all my precious possessions with specific catalogues during specific seasons. Things you can't possibly find anymore fill my apartment. I can't let the hours I stood in line for limited pieces go to waste. They're one of a kind. They'll never be made again. I can't bear to lose any. My possessions in sort represent my hard work. The more I worked, the more I could afford them.

Images of my priceless possessions flew by and suddenly I became brave. Brave enough to kick my blanket away and take a hold of an object I deem would make the most damage. A lighter. I kept one in the drawer of my bedside table—nowadays, only for candles. A lighter may be small, but with a click, it can harm anything for the exception of water.

What would have been even better is a cellphone. With that, I could've called the police and there would be no need to be brave. Alas, I forgot my phone in the living room.

With an alert mind, I tiptoed my way to the door and placed my ear on it. Despite having a lighter in my hand, I'm scared out of my wits. The same rustling was heard until another type of sound was added. Dangling. This time, it's dangling. Jewellery clashing with each other. This thief is taking my jewellery! No more tiptoeing. I barged out of my room and pressed the lighter on. I brought the flame forward to see the thief. I'm faced with a pair of clear blue eyes peeking out of a crystal mask. Out of shock, I turn off the lighter, bringing me back to total darkness. My intermission sure has ended, but another type of show began. One beyond my expectations.

I brought the flame back since out of sight, out of mind, doesn't work in this situation.

Those blue eyes stare into mine without a word. My eyes can't leave the thief for more reasons than the fact he is a thief. I moved the flame around and observed his mask and every little crystal glued on. Strings full of crystals veiled down his every feature. I'm no expert, but they look authentic. The mask shines brighter than any of my jewellery.

"You're the Crystal Mask," I was able to say.

He doesn't budge or part his lips to speak. His quickened breath is all that reached my ears.

This might be a weird thought to have while in peril, but should I feel honoured that the Crystal Mask—a thief targeting the rich—visited me. I should be terrified and I am. But confirmation doesn't feel so bad. I never thought of myself as filthy rich—yet. Compared to the richest people in Mardi Town, I'm a sprout while they're majestic trees with an infinite amount of fruits growing out. Intrusive thought aside, a freaking wanted criminal is in my house and the only thing I've done is call his name. I haven't yelled or ran away. I could throw my lighter at him, but that could potentially leave me homeless and liable for fire damage.

"Say something!" I say in a frenzy.

Like me, the thief hasn't moved. His feet are stuck on the floor. The only movements in the room are the dangling crystals of his mask and the flame of my lighter.

This man is the most foolish robber one could encounter. The crystals dangling from the mask hit each other—therefore produce noise—and reflect light on the walls. The cherry on top, though, is the perfume he wears. A strong scent of musk occupies the room. There's no doubt he wore the mask and perfume on purpose. Why else would he be so noticeable in a place you'd want to leave unnoticed? What bothers me is that if he truly was foolish, he'd already be behind bars.

My senses coming back, I tell him: "Drop whatever you're holding."

I wanted to approach with my flame that is barely holding on from being lit for so long, but even I can get petrified. Simultaneously, I am captivated by his eyes. The crystals might appear authentic, but the blue in his eyes doesn't. Just as I stared deeper, his eyes fell down to his hand. I followed as he released his fist and let what he held fall down. The sound was lighter than anticipated and lowering the lighter, I could see papers falling. This could be worrying.

"That's it?" I say, my eyes back to his.

I didn't keep cash in my apartment with the exception of a couple of bills in my wallet for emergency. That amount, though, was not worth fussing about.

His breath is the sole response I seem to get. Having said that, I'm not sure if breathing counts as an answer. He'd die if he stopped.

The pace of the breath slowed; I'd almost think him relaxed. Why would he be? He's caught red-handed and had to relinquish his newly acquired goods. Why doesn't he look worried?

He brought forth his hands—covered by black leather gloves—and ever so clearly displayed his empty palms.

"You're not here for expensive objects?" I ask, in a rather naïve tone.

The man nodded in denial, the strings of

crystals moving along right to left.

"Why have you come, then?"

This question can't be answered with a yes or a no. He can try, but I'll understand nothing of it.

A slight squint of his eye and he at last moved. Yet this movement wasn't one I'd wanted. With rushed feet, he took off. I had to blink a few times to take in what had just happened. Then, in no time, I ran after him. As I followed him out of my apartment, my lighter had the audacity to turn off—the fuel ran out. Is it worth it to chase after a dangerous man who, fortunately wasn't able to steal a thing? Let alone the fact that my feet are bare. With nothing in sight, I ceased to run and stood in darkness, the scent of his musk perfume lingering in the air.

Chapter 8

I fiddled with the handle of my coffee mug—I don't always drink espressos —and said: "The Crystal Mask came by my house last night."

Robert dropped the glass he wiped and looked up.

"Please explain," he said, straining to keep his expression under control.

Robert's the type of person who likes to hear all the details before reacting.

"I heard a sound at 3 in the morning. I went out to the living room and saw him."

And I'm the type that gives out brief

explanations. I'll admit that I do it on purpose with Robert. It's my greed to get some reactions out of him.

"Did he hurt you? Did he steal?" he said, hiding the words *elaborate please.*

"I think I caught him too early on. He didn't have the chance to steal and ran off on his own after a while."

"After a while?" Robert raised an eyebrow.

"I talked to him, but he didn't say a thing. He answered using head gestures. When I asked a question he couldn't gesture a response to, he sprinted away."

"Good," he said, going back to cleaning his glass.

Not even the Crystal Mask was able to provoke a reaction out of him.

"I wonder if I should go to the police?" I then said.

That is when he let himself go. He slammed the counter before raising a hand to his forehead, which was full of lines.

"You mean to tell me you haven't already? You're telling me before the police?" he said and I could almost swear his eyes turned fire red.

"Nothing was stolen. I'm not sure what to report..." As I spoke, I realized how stupid this sounds.

"Uh. I don't know, maybe trespassing? That's illegal." His tone was justifiably passive aggressive.

He grabbed my empty cup. I suspect he was fed up with my fidgeting.

"You're right. He did enter without permission."

"It's more than without permission. He broke in. You're a victim and a witness. You'll be of some help to the investigation. It's possible for the Crystal Mask to return and complete the job. You need to tell the police."

"I have no choice then."

His lips pressed tight into a grimace. Robert is back at suppressing whatever he is feeling in there. All I can do is guess. Now, I'm guessing he's in disbelief. How could she be this idiotic to not even consider getting help from the police?

I agree, Robert. To excuse my idiotic self, I'd like to say that I was still processing the events of last night. I couldn't get a wink of sleep afterwards. The remaining of my night was spent in the corner of my living room staring aimlessly at the dark. I'd locked my door—though that didn't stop him before. For some reason, I didn't fear he'd come back because my intuition trusted he wouldn't.

Fear wasn't what kept me awake. It was an utter daze. Till now, I hadn't snapped out of it.

The image of the crystal-mask-wearing man is stuck in my mind as if I were hypnotized to.

Is that the reason he wears the mask? To engrave it into his victim's memory. But a thief wouldn't carry such intention. He'd avoid getting caught at all costs. Yesterday was his second mishap. He's known by the public because someone witnessed him before me.

Robert filled my travel mug with coffee before handing it to me.

"Promise me you'll go straight to the police. Surely they'll offer you some sort of protection."

When he was talking, he deliberately avoided making eye contact with me. The last thing he'd want to do is expose how worried he is.

"I'm on my way."

I'm thankful to have someone like Robert in my life. He's a father figure to me as much as he is a friend. My real father shares nothing in common with Robert. If we are to reincarnate, I wish to be re-born as his daughter or, at the very least, his friend. If that were the case, I'd lead a good life from the start.

***

I attempt to warm my hands with the mug that is filled to the brim with burning hot coffee with no success. The heat doesn't seep in the outside. And to drink the coffee now would only burn my mouth. To leave it open will cool down the coffee rather quickly since it's freezing outside. Ultimately, it would beat the purpose of a travel mug to keep the coffee warm. None of this really matters, since the police station itself isn't far. The station is in between Java Haze on Late Street and the bank on Soul Street. It's right at the crossroad.

Getting rid of my useless thoughts concerning coffee, I found myself in front of the station, at last. I didn't hesitate to step in knowing there's a functioning heater there. February's always the coldest month of the year and I hate it.

I scanned for an empty desk. All were respectively filled with an officer and a civilian. The day appears to be busy. Were there this many incidents in Mardi Town? These people might be here for minor occurrences or for documentation. That would make more sense. I bet I have the most pertinent story of the day. Not that the story's praise worthy. Robert would scream if he heard my thoughts.

Not losing time, I sat at the one empty desk I found. This one didn't have an officer sitting by the other end. And unlike a cash register, there wasn't a bell to ring. Patience is a virtue while time is money. With crossed legs, I tapped my nail against the edge of the chair steadily. For my mind to not go in other ways, I distract it with fidgeting. And before I knew it, an officer walked my way.

"I am sorry for the delay," he said, prior to settling into his cushioned seat.

"It's alright." I said, truths be said, it's not alright, but they must be up to their ears with cases today—judging by the number of people.

Apart from the tardiness, another issue caught my eye. Particularly, it's the officer that caught my eye. How is it that he appears familiar when I've never seen him before? Have I? If he feels familiar, then I must have seen him somewhere. This diamond shaped face. These wide cheekbones. This narrow chin. These prominent eyes. This roman nose. These wide and down turned lips. This otherworldly face where the features are all large scaled, yet they don't overwhelm one another. I just can't pinpoint where I'd caught sight of him.

All this time, I'd been staring without a word. The officer's so kind and patient he hasn't mentioned it.

"Um, I'm here to report a near burglary."

"Near?"

"Yes, I think the Crystal mask came to my apartment last night."

Now for the astounded expression. The 'What did you say?' expression.

"You think?" he asked, ever so calmly.

Not what I expected, but alright.

I told the officer I thought it was the Crystal Mask, because while everything checked the mark—robbery, mask made of crystal, etc—there's a possibility for the mask to be fake. The man of last night could be a copycat. Of course, there's no way I would've gotten confirmation from the man himself. It seems reasonable to assume instead of being entirely confident.

"I saw him in my apartment, wearing a crystal mask. That is why I think it's possible for him to have been the Crystal Mask."

After a few mouse clicks, he began typing on the computer.

"I'll start a report, but I have a few questions for you. You see, we've gotten quite the reports on him and it gets hard to discern the truth. I hope you have the time to answer all the questions. They were made to ensure the right information goes towards his file."

I should be offended by his assumption that I'm lying from the start. But they must truly have gotten plenty of make believe reports from people seeking entertainment. Hearing that, I can't blame him for making a whole questionnaire. Besides, there's a mug of coffee in my hand and a heater in the station. I can afford to spend some time.

"Let us start the questionnaire," I said in

my turn.

There's nothing to be afraid of when I know what I saw.

"Accordingly, we'll start with your full name and address."

Basics first, roger that.

"Rene Mint. 1030 Darling avenue, 11th floor, 3rd unit."

"I've heard of you, Miss Mint. Are you the successful young business woman that took Mardi Town by storm?"

"Someone seems to disagree with that statement. He's a very aggravating person at that," I said with a frown. While even a police officer associated my name with success, Avel, that man, remains the only one who deems otherwise.

"Could you describe last night's event and be as descriptive as you can be?"

The moment I'd spent last night felt lengthy, while in reality, it was nothing but brief. Despite it having been a marking event, the details started to fade in my memory.

When telling the officer what I

witnessed, I soon discovered that words alone could not describe the outlandish moment that was last night. My description was the simplest.

"Did he leave something behind?" he asked.

"I don't suppose so. I haven't noticed anything new or missing. On other thoughts, there is something, but it isn't an object."

He typed with rapid hands, at the same time, he maintained eye contact.

"If not, then?"

"The scent of his cologne. I'm sure it's still lingering in the air of my living room. He smells like musk."

"Interesting."

"Isn't it?"

"Aside from the mask and the perfume, was there an element that stood out?"

"With the small flame of a lighter, there wasn't much I could see. And the mask itself was so mesmerizing, you'd find it hard to look elsewhere."

"In other words, you've seen nothing

else?"

"That is right."

As he typed some more, my instincts grew louder. There's no doubt I've seen him somewhere, yet where? There's no way to know unless I ask. And obviously, there's nothing wrong with asking.

Thus, I did.

"I'm sorry, but I just have to ask. Have we met somewhere? You look familiar."

"Have we?" he said, a grin appearing on his face.

"We have. Haven't we? It's driving me crazy how I can't remember."

"I did look very different that night."

That night? Different? His hint passed over my head.

"What do you mean, you looked different?"

He took his hands off the keyboard and drew his chair forward for his face to be near mine.

In a whisper, he said: "The club."

This word triggered back the memories of my clubbing night. Images of the white-haired man associated with the officer in front of me. Indeed. This man is the one I found to have a unique style at the club. It never crossed my mind that I would meet him once more, or that he would be a police officer.

On another note, how does he know?

"You noticed me too, it seems," I said.

I must've not been the only one who experienced a sense of connection.

"Yes, yes," he said, nodding and drawing farther anew. "I recognized my intentions in your dance."

"What did you think were my intentions?"

"To release stress caused by anger?"

"Bingo!" I exclaimed, snapping a finger.

He smiled a kind smile, with eyes creasing downwards.

"That night was right before the Crystal Mask's visit. You must be having some kind of week," he added.

"Truths be told, the concern that led me to the club is bigger than a measly attempted robbery. I know a man more infuriating than the Crystal Mask."

Merely thinking of him is enough to bring back the anger I fought so hard to release at the club. He renders my coping mechanism useless.

"I do as well," the officer said, surprising me. "A man that troubles me and makes life harder than it already is."

Welcome to the club, officer whose name I don't know.

"Miss Rene, even if you consider the attempted robbery of less importance, you should still be careful. Your house is prone to another visit from the Crystal Mask," he said, going back to his duties of policeman. I suspect he was brought back to his secret identity for a moment when recalling the night where he was free.

"I'll be fine," I said, without dwelling on it.

"We don't want to risk a thing."

"What should I do then to be careful? He broke through my lock."

"Perhaps stay with someone you know, temporarily, and or change your lock to a more secure one. The police force can also provide you with protection."

The options come across as overbearing. Why would I leave my home for who knows how long? I couldn't do this to someone, nor could I do it to myself. My space is my own, that goes as well for my boundaries. I grew comfortable to living alone. The experience turned out better than I imagined. Trust me when I say I imagined how well I would be in a place belonging to only me. I dreamed of it every day until the day it became true. I won't walk out, nor will I let the police invade my circle for a petty thief that doesn't appear too dangerous.

"Changing my lock is all I can accept," I told him.

"As you like. Know that if you ever change your mind, the station's always open."

"I understand."

I understood, but I hope he won't count on my visit.

"One last thing. You might receive calls

from the station, don't ignore them. You can refuse police protection, but you can't refuse follow-up calls," he said, a hint of playfulness in his voice.

"Sure, sure. I can accommodate a few calls."

"Then that'll be it, Miss Rene. We are working hard to find that criminal."

Criminal, he said. It's always funny to see how people from different sides view him. To the rich, he's the enemy. I'm sure a few couldn't even report him if he stole goods purchased illegally. To the common class, he's a conflicting being. Should they view him as refreshing or maintain the perception that his methods are wrong? To the less fortunate, he might be a hero that has made great changes to the quality of their lives. To the police, he is a criminal they need to find for order in the town. To me, he is... A validation I'm rich enough to be visited by the Crystal Mask.

Chapter 9

Life goes on, doesn't it? Lunch reaches, and I'd go eat with Auburn in her office. I would. But the tension between us hasn't eased. I fear that I might be the only one with tension. If I were to face Auburn, I don't know how I'll act. Would I be able to pretend I'm not mad? Time and space might do the trick to either resolve the conflict or give me the energy to confront her. Surely we'll resolve the misunderstanding at some point. Then, the same old routine we love so dearly will come back.

After departing from the police station, I

walked past the bank. That building triggers thoughts full of hatred. All pointed at Avel rather than the bank itself. The image of his blank face haunts me. But speaking of the devil. As though my head printed his image on the asphalt, Avel walked out of the bank. The time just happened to be two o'clock, and that just happened to be his coffee break.

"Avel!" I call, taking the few steps I needed to catch up.

I didn't eat lunch yet, but I could go for a coffee first.

"Perchance, are you stalking me?" he said with a clenched jaw.

"You don't believe in destiny?"

"The police station is right there. I can report you right this instant," he said, pointing a finger at the station.

"They'll laugh at you," I replied, laughing myself.

"Why would they?"

"Because an officer there is my alibi. I'm on my way back from reporting an incident."

"Then go on to your destination. We're not acquaintances. If you bump into someone you don't know, you keep on walking," he said, a vein in his neck throbbing.

I'm not surprised he didn't ask about my report. He lacks the emotion of interest. I'd be surprised if he did ask.

"You're breaking my heart," I said, placing two hands near my heart. "After having met a couple of times, I thought we were becoming friends."

With enough jokes he could open up.

"Friends?" he scoffed, his mouth lopsided and his eyes nearly popping out.

We can call this a sign. A sign that I bring out expressions out of him. Many people seem reserved, but then their true colours show in front of the very few people close to them.

He continued: "Must you ruin this coffee break too?"

"Now, now, Avel. Haven't they taught you that lying is an ill quality? You had more fun playing a round of rummy with me rather than playing the solitaire by yourself. No?"

"Your guess is wrong," he said, his posture closing.

"I didn't guess," I then had to answer, with a firmer tone.

Walking ahead, I'm confident he'll follow, as there is no other path to Java Haze. Where else would he go when he's a Java Haze regular who's perhaps not once changed locations for his 2 o'clock coffee break?

He was silent in following me with only the sound of his Chelsea boots crushing the snow. The annoyance on his face gives off another sound, which is music to my ears. Like edgy strokes of an electric guitar. This satisfaction is turning into an addiction. I guess keeping your friends close and your enemies closer is more fun than it sounds. I'd love to poke him some more, but then I'd be risking the premature end of my mission. The rope I have around him is so thin it's threatening to break.

To relieve my boredom, I settled with

watching his feet and mimicking their pace. The game was amusing until Avel noticed and sent me a death glare with those cold eyes of his. I shivered because of the cold, not his glare. I hope he understands that. Considering all the bickering we've done, I'm better off not saying a thing. I fear we'll keep at it all day if I add on.

This time, I'll be focused and professional. I'll mention the loan. If I'm too engrossed in the game to remember it again, my future looks bleak. This lingering thought led to a few more that could cause this bleak future. The derailing friendship I share with Auburn. The looming threat of a second visit from the Crystal Mask. The pile of work I'll need to keep performing if I don't purchase a house.

I'm starting to wonder if playing cards with this man is even worth the time? That's it. I'm betting all my chances on this round. The fire in me is burning.

Without delay I shouted, "Let's get this done!" forgetting that I wasn't walking alone, in consequences, I startled him.

"Sure, let's get this done," he repeated in a feeble voice, lacking 110% of my enthusiasm. That's Avel for you—not that I'm gradually grasping his personality. I have no intention of doing so.

"One thing," he then started to say, "Don't raise your expectations. We'll play a game of cards and that's all. Nothing you say will change my decision on your loan."

Says the man who's giving me an open mic.

Maybe he really enjoys playing cards with someone else. Most precisely me. He discovered in him something called competitiveness. Let me tell you that once found, this emotion sticks to you like honey.

"Persistence is worth its weigh in gold," I told him, my feet eager to reach the café.

"You missed your vocation. You should have become a writer. Then you wouldn't need this loan and we'd never have met."

"And you should have become a critic. Then all your nonsensical critics would be justifiable. I'd think: Oh, this man's job is to critic, of course he's gonna spend his day at it."

I made the man chuckle. I repeat. He laughed. I couldn't help but stare as he threw his head back and emitted waves of hearty laughter. His eyes sparkled like they regained glimmer for the first time in years. I find myself curious about the kind of person he was before. The lines creasing next to his eyes when he laughs show he'd laughed quite a bit before. He wasn't forever cold.

***

Please let me get the three of diamonds, I prayed to the god of cards. My shoulders fell the moment I saw the card I drew. I can't hide the disappointment when a useless four of hearts comes up. The only one I need is the three of diamonds.

Yes, I appear to be failing once more at

my attempt to bargain. The game makes me lose my speech, and strategies occupy most of my head. Should I keep this card? Should I get rid of this one? Please let this card be the one... Did he already win? Is he going to place this card faced down and declare victory? Not yet? Then I can still win. On and on, these thoughts turn around.

Thankfully, I have an ally in this coffee shop. Robert came to tap on my shoulder.

He whispered in my ear, "don't forget your goal."

I must've been so quiet he knew I'd forgotten about my mission. I nearly slapped myself hearing his wise words, but then Avel spoke up.

"Focus on the game," he said, his gaze fixed on the cards. He must have heard Robert's whisper. "If you win, I'll give you a chance to sell your idea."

Does he think of himself as a god to give me a chance?

"You're on, Avel."

I accepted his offer, regardless of the wound inflicted on my pride.

"Why do you keep on using my first name?"

"There's no particular reason, really."

"If there's no reason, could you stop?"

He's nice enough to ask, but I'm not as nice to stop.

"What should I call you then? Mr. Malt feels too distant."

"I don't recall us being close at all."

"We'll see each other much too often for you to repeat that disk, Avel," I said, my tongue lingering on the roof of my mouth, elongating the last syllable of his name. "You can call be by my name too, you know?" I said, realizing he hadn't called me by my name since we'd met at the bank.

"Like hell I will," he said, his hands briefly clenching before throwing a three of diamonds.

If this was poker, I'd be the worst player since I can't hide my smile. Sadly for Avel, it's game over. I lay down my suites and runs, including the precious three of diamonds.

"Checkmate," I said, knowing that only applies to chess.

I couldn't find a more satisfying term.

"You have 10 minutes, Rene," he said, enunciating both syllables of my name with succulence.

A glare couldn't give me shivers, but this has done it. Down every line of my spine. He brought all the cards into a pile while I processed how he'd called my name and how purposefully he did.

"The clock is ticking, Rene." Again.

How funny he must think he is.

Clearing my throat, I brought my attention back to what matters most: business.

"I've thought about what you said long enough to understand it didn't make sense. You said my business's young and unstable. I agree with the former, not the latter. If per minuscule, almost zero chance I am unable to pay the loan anymore, you'll just have to seize the million dollar house. You won't have any loss then."

He tapped a finger on the table, continuously as he prepared to speak.

"Most times, we'd want to avoid going this far. It takes time and money to sell a house. The time itself it takes could bring a loss for the bank."

I almost stood out of frustration.

"How hard can a gorgeous and expensive house be to sell?"

In contrast to the tension in my voice, Avel appeared calm. He settled into his chair as if it were a sofa in his living room.

"You said it yourself. The house is expensive. Not everyone can afford it. Even you, Ms. Mint, need a loan at the moment."

I wouldn't have needed a loan if I hadn't spent my newly earned money without a budget or a simple stop sign. I'm the one to blame, I know. I'm the reason for my misfortune, I know. But there is always a Plan B and for that one, Avel is to blame. But blaming does nothing with a man that doesn't feel the least bit apologetic?

"Instead of refusing and denying, can't you give me advice for me to improve and bring you a file worth approving?"

"Time and consistent growth are all you need. If in a year your business is still going well, come see me at the bank," he said, drinking the last of his coffee.

One year? Just like Robert said. The day I envisioned myself owning a house and only having to manage this one house is the day my work turned taxing. I had a taste of a better life—in a daydream. How could I keep drinking instant coffee after tasting exquisite espressos? Same thing.

With a mere few minutes left, I had to try something.

"Do you know me from elsewhere? Did you hear rumours about me?"

He gazed at me with sudden focus.

In the past that I left behind, many disliked me enough to spread false rumours. Seeing that the world is smaller than it seems, the possibility for him to have met me or someone I knew before isn't zero. Were that possibility true, things would clear up.

"The only place I'd seen you prior our

meeting at the bank is here, Java Haze," he said.

No words are left to say beyond this. I won a measly round of rummy while he won the actual game I've been dying to win. Misery sure loves its company. We both lost what interested us most and won what mattered little to us.

His finger tapping on the table slowed down, yet didn't halt.

"Time's ticking, Rene. Nothing more to say?"

How aggravating.

I bit my lip, the fingers on my lap curling.

"No," I said, my voice barely audible.

"Time's up then."

Avel stood to wear his wool coat, the colour of charcoal. "I'll see you in a year. If you're still holding on," he felt the need to add with a smirk.

Oh, how I want to wipe that smirk off his face and replace it with a frown, followed by a heavy stream of tears.

If I do end up visiting him next year, I

know that with a smug face he'll say something such as 'you see. I told you that time was the solution to all your problems. I was the one to give you that solution because I am always right. From now on, call me Mr. Right.'

This might be an exaggeration since he is a man of little words. Though I'm sure his face will say these words without a sound. He'll think it in the most condescending way, and that angers me the same.

"See you in a year," he said, buttoning his coat.

"We'll see about that," I muttered under my breath.

He left in what I can imagine is a happy stride. He knows there's nothing left for me to say.

The bargaining stage is done. To end on this note feels so wrong. I didn't change his mind in the least. This loan is officially beyond my control. That alone is disappointing because I feel I haven't done enough.

These rounds of banter and rummy were fun when I had a glimmer of hope in mind. They even leave me to imagine an alternate reality where Avel and I could have met amicably at Java Haze and played cards once in a while. In this reality, neither Avel nor I would agree to another round. If it weren't for the loan, I would have settled for the counter that day.

Chapter 10

The night after, I'd fallen asleep for the mere reason I lacked sleep from previous nights. My problems, though, didn't fail to wake me up in time for the sunrise. So I obliged and stared at the rising sun. How did it get this bad? There's no way I'll fall into the next stages: depression and acceptance. Those don't go well with my mindset and I'll make sure they'll never see the light.

Instead, I'm the one to see the light. The light reflected in Auburn's eyes.

After our call, Laine had a conversation with Auburn, and I imagine she sensed the underlying tension between us. Thus, here we are in my bedroom, having some sort of staring contest. I sat on the velvet green sheets of my bed while Auburn sat on my reading chair facing the city view. Laine sat on a cushion on the floor between us. She chose to sit there herself to show she was unbiased. I sure hope she is unbiased because she's only heard one side of the story, Auburn's. We haven't discussed the lunch incident where Auburn talked a bit weird, or the fact that lunch didn't happen yesterday. I never meant for it to become a big deal. What is one missed lunch?

None said a word since stepping inside. The room is so calm, I can pick up the ticking of Laine's watch.

I stared at Auburn, who'd fixed her gaze out the window since long. Poor Laine twisted her neck to look at both of us equally.

"Why did you call us here?" Auburn then said in a tone I couldn't recognize. It was so bleak.

In truth, I was the one to call this

meeting. If the loan was unattainable, I thought I'd at least work on saving other parts of my life. It's hard to imagine spending another year of hardships without the support of my best friends. There's so much complaining I'll want to do. So many overly sweet cakes I'll want to eat with them for the morale. I'll need so many more unofficial therapy sessions with Laine. They are people I don't think I can live without anymore. For the longest time, I thought, once a lonely soul, always a lonely soul. They proved me wrong in the most glorious way.

"To solve misunderstandings," I said for both Auburn and Laine to hear.

Of course, I have no conflict with Laine, but they're a set. They were best friends before meeting me. I can't be the one to split such a precious friendship.

"What's there to solve?" Auburn had said.

It's challenging to grasp how she managed to say it so calmly. What do you mean there's nothing to solve?

"We haven't talked in a while. Don't you find that strange?" I then said.

"You were the one that didn't come eat lunch with me."

"I never promised I'd come every day. Besides, you haven't called asking why I didn't come. Now you're upset about it?"

Auburn and I called each other daily, spouting nonsense. Entertaining nonsense. We basically shared the same brain cells. Lately, she hasn't called me much, and I didn't either. I assumed she felt guilty because of our recent conversations. However, I now know it isn't the case. She fell into the trap of victim mentality. She didn't ask herself: Did I do something to upset her? No. She considered in her mind: Rene's done me wrong. And nothing else.

"See, it's all a misunderstanding," Laine said in turn.

I wonder of what she'd heard from Auburn. Yet I'm sure the story's very one-sided.

"I don't see it," Auburn said, hiding her face deeper into the window. That makes it hard to see what kind of expression she has on.

"You both assumed the other was busy and didn't call to ask about lunch. A complete misunderstanding," Laine added, a hopeful smile on her face.

"It wasn't a misunderstanding," I had the urge to say. "I was first to be upset. Auburn, you didn't call me because you knew you'd been harsh these days. I wanted to give you time."

Hearing that, she turned to us, her forehead creased.

"I did not!" she jabbed.

"You still stand on everything you said?" I asked, my lack of sleep affecting my emotions. The lower my energy levels are, the more dramatic and easily offended I get.

"I do."

"What did she say?" Laine said, peeking in our range of vision.

I'm sure of it now. Auburn honeyed her words and spiced mine when she talked with Laine.

"She practically cursed my business and took the side of a man she's never met over her best friend!"

"I didn't curse your business. I said you can expect highs and lows."

"You said rising so quickly could foreshadow a rapid descent. That's not normal highs and lows that's bankruptcy!"

What angers me most isn't the curse. No, it's much more. She's my best friend. I went to see her to rant not to make her convince Avel. I'd only wanted her to agree with me. To comfort me. To curse Avel with me. For the fun of it.

"I simply said that man was right, and you're saying I'm on his side," she mumbled.

"Agreeing with my enemy is the last thing you should do as a best friend."

I might have been so obsessed with the idea of a perfect best friend that I lost touch with reality. The perfect best friend doesn't exist.

She looked at me straight in the eyes with a sharp gaze, "You sure made him an enemy fast. So what? A person tells you no for once, and they're the devil now? I guess your family never refused you anything growing up."

I believed I'd turn my life around enough by meeting wonderful friends in a marvellous town. It appears I was wrong. My fantasies of friendship are now shattered in so many pieces it'd be hard to find them all, let alone glue them back. Wouldn't Auburn know I didn't come from money? I came here not a penny to my name. Though I never told her of my past, it wouldn't be hard to guess there were no rainbows in my life. If I did come from a happy family, wouldn't I talk about it whenever an opportunity arised?

"Calm down, Auburn," Laine said— knowing my origin story. "And Rene, don't get mad."

A bit too late for that. I tighten my fist in an attempt to suppress my outrage. My nails press against my palm; it doesn't hurt much compared to the ache in my heart. I sense an ending. I feel this conversation being irreversible.

"You're going too far," I said in a quieter voice. "Why do people assume my money isn't my own? Is it so hard to imagine that a young person earned a significant fortune on her own? You shouldn't assume. That's wrong. To assume allows you to predict. If your prediction is wrong, that leads to a fair amount of disappointment. I'm not who you think I am. Did you always believe I hid my powerful secrets?"

Maybe Auburn is just disappointed that what I have to hide is not a secret rich family. That may be it.

I caught a glimpse of Laine. She seems to have given up. Her shoulders are dropping and her eyes no longer move relentlessly from side to side. I hope she doesn't decide to change career paths because of us.

"It's hard to understand what you're talking about," Auburn then said.

I could spill the truth. Tell her everything I vowed to never talk about—for my own good. I wanted to trick my brain into thinking it never happened. I thought never talking about it would bury the story, and you don't unearth what you buried underground. With the exception of a time capsule but that's not what I had in mind. I thought of the past years as a dead person.

Auburn lost my trust. There's no need to consider enlightening her.

Given that I didn't answer, she continued: "You came here out of the blue, a year and a half ago. What's so secret you need to hide it? Was your father a rich con man that got caught? Did you follow his footsteps to ruin Mardi Town? I wouldn't even be surprised if I heard you were working with the Crystal Mask."

My blood boiled hearing her run her mouth. She knows nothing, and acts like I've stolen the world from under her palm.

Who is this person in front of me?

"At this point, I wish all you said was true. Then my life would have been easier." I began to feel tears welling up. Tears I swore to never show a soul anymore. "We've been friends for long enough and all you are doing now is confronting me with suspicions I'm sure you've had since the day you met me. Why did it take so long for you to ask? Did you pretend to be my friend out of curiosity? Did you suppose I'd come clean one day saying that, in fact, my family is very rich and since you've been a loyal friend, I'll take you in and make you taste abundance?"

Tears betrayed me as they streamed down my cheeks. "I don't get it, Auburn. I don't."

She looked at me, her eyes fleeing my tears. Her forehead creased more as if she were more angry than before. I gazed away —not wanting to imprint the blurry image of her angered face in my memory. It's not an image I want to be reminded of for long.

My gaze switched to Laine, who appeared hesitant. She seemed ready to spring off her feet, but where? If she were to comfort me, Auburn would consider it a betrayal and likewise if she'd done the opposite. Laine is our friend before she is a therapist. I understand things must be hard in the middle. That said, I wouldn't mind it so much if she were to lend a hand to Auburn. They've known each other longer. Their relation is deeper. I couldn't be worth jeopardizing an old friendship.

If I wished for Laine to come to me, that would be selfish. I'm likely better off on my own, and they're better off together—without a bratty rich girl.

No matter how much I want to storm out of the place, there's no getaway—this is my home. And who am I to kick them out? I won't blame them for walking it out on me. In part, that's what I deserve. To imagine I could completely start anew was reaching for the moon. At least with the fortune I amassed, I could say that I landed among the stars. And that should have been enough for me. It's not too late to content myself with it.

"Let's not get carried away," Laine spoke with a sigh as she found the courage to speak.

"I'll get going," Auburn said, sparing me the need to ask myself.

She stood from the reading chair and made her way to the door. Laine looked at me with concern. I nodded to tell her it's fine.

"I'd rather be alone. Go with Auburn. She'll need you more."

"Are you sure?"

"I'm sure."

"I don't believe this is right," she said, walking towards my bed. "You shouldn't be alone right now."

I stood, not letting her sit beside me—it'd take longer to bring her out then.

"Be with Auburn. I won't be mad. I'll be alone but not lonely. I truly need this time, so please go."

I couldn't ever be mean to Laine. Contrary to Auburn, she is a good friend. If I'd met her, and she had no other best friend, perhaps those fantasies could have been real for longer.

"Let me do one thing," she said, heading out of the room.

I followed her until she stopped near the cabinets in the kitchen.

"For precautions," she said, taking my bottle of whisky. "I'll bring it back to you when the problem's resolved."

I gave her the small smile I could still give. Yet I fear there won't be a resolution when there's no will.

Now I'm alone in an apartment that feels wider than usual. I'm left with space and a scent of musk that doesn't seem to disappear.

Chapter 11

Why do I feel hangover when not a drop of alcohol entered my system last night? This morning's already a mess. My hair's tangled and rising like a lion's. My face is bloated like a marshmallow. The bags under my eyes are a new shade of purple. I nearly threw my phone away when I looked at myself in the camera. And last but not least, my back is aching as if I'd carried bricks yesterday. It's the result of tossing and turning all night. Today again, I beat my alarm and awoke earlier. Poor thing lost its only job.

By now, you'd know sleepless nights

won't be my downfall. Not much is needed to fix all of those petty problems. Each has a solution.

The expensive hair products I own aren't for show, they're for bad hair day battles. If I end my shower with cold water, I'll ease my back pain. The spoons I keep in my freezer at all times will reduce the puffiness on my face. For the purple bags, I suppose I'll rock the mysterious woman exhausted by her problems look. I don't believe in covering what's natural.

After the emergency repairs, I was ready to go outside. Staying too long in an apartment that won't be visited any time soon is bound to make me depressed. I'm not much of a homebody.

Right after going down the stairs, I thought about checking the mail. Surely there's something. Perhaps that something will brighten up my day. Sometimes you find yourself expecting the unexpected. A paradox, isn't it? I think it's hope. Hope that someone has your back and or that your day will magically get better.

Upon opening my mailbox, I found a single letter. One that nearly blended with the interior being pitch black. What made it stand out is the red wax seal in the middle. I quickly noticed there was no from address nor was there my address printed on it. The sender must have hand-delivered it then. Could be an elaborate marketing strategy or, worse, a secret admirer. I wasted no time in breaking the seal. The letter itself was handwritten in fancy lettering as though it was written with a fountain pen. Colour me intrigued.

It read:

Dear Rene Mint,

You are cordially invited to a series of exclusive meetings concerning the Crystal Mask. We were informed of your encounter with the Crystal Mask and thought it appropriate to reach an invitation out.

We hope to gather alike individuals carrying a same goal. By combining our strengths we could certainly bring results the police have failed to deliver.

As stated previously, the meetings are

exclusive therefore, they must remain confidential. You mustn't speak of this letter nor the identity of the people you'll meet during the meetings. For your safety and others, please keep the information to yourself.

As for the details, every gathering will occur when the clock strikes at midnight. The locations and dates are X, they constantly change. We'll never speak at the same table twice to lessen the risks associated with our private meetings. You'll be able to learn of the date and location through letters such as this one.

The last detail I need to mention is the assignment of partners. During the first gathering, you'll make the arrangements together. The inclusion of partners will enable secretive communication and advancements in between the official meetings, which will be limited as a precautionary measure. I trust you'll find a creative way to assign partners.

I hope you are willing to take a chance in this affair. Together we will find the

Crystal Mask who has been terrorizing the town.

P.S. February the 11th at the Firefly elementary school [classroom 6-B]

Best Regards

No name was signed on the bottom, leaving me confused. I kept staring at the same words until they'd lost all meaning. This letter came out straight out of a mystery novel, and now I'm part of that mystery novel. That is, if I choose to attend. But of course I am. I'm not sure that I share the same goals as the others or even a goal at all. The image of the Crystal Mask sure is stuck in my mind, but it's not terrorizing me. The last line of the letter doesn't make too much sense. Is he really terrorizing the town? He's gained the favour of the general public. The victims are ones that can afford a dent in their wallet. The dent must be the size of a pea.

Regardless, his activities are criminal and that is a fact I can't help but agree with. There has to be other ways to aid the community without resorting to stealing.

I nearly became a victim myself—one that would've suffered from the dent in her wallet—yet I find myself wanting to stay neutral. In a place where there is nothing to admit.

Going back to the letter, isn't it odd that they chose for us to meet at an elementary school? Out of all places. Sure nobody roams there at midnight. I guess I'm just disappointed by the choice of location. The language in the letter was rather sophisticated. The people attending are filthy rich, so much so that they wouldn't need a loan to buy a million dollars house. Their winter cabin would cost more.

Maybe I'll be out of place as I did many times before. Perhaps even now I'm starting to feel out of place. I could say that my place is lost. My sense of belonging came with the friendships I gained. I belonged amongst the first people I thought dear to me. But no longer.

Despite my money, the solitary lifestyle doesn't change. I was too quick to judge Avel by saying he played the solitaire like the loner he is. Looks like I'll be doing the same from now on. Now, back under my rock, I'll have to be content with money only. I'll tell myself that it is different from the past. If I were to be sad, I can shop, I can drink as many coffees as I want and buy pastries in bulk, knowing my pockets can withstand far more. Wouldn't that be enough to make me happy? Wouldn't money be sufficient?

All these thoughts about being out-of-place make me unsure of this secret meeting. They sent an invitation because a rat leaked my report and the Crystal Mask clearly came to my house by mistake. He too probably heard the rumours I'm old money. How disappointed he must be to have seen my house. He would've come out nearly empty-handed even if I hadn't caught him. The other victims had all been CEOs from established companies. In other words, giants of Mardi Town. My income to them is their children's pocket money.

Inferiority isn't the sole reason I'm hesitating. The meeting itself is strange.

There's no hint as to who organized it and it appears the police aren't involved. Not officially, at least. The courage it takes to invite rich and powerful people means they're just as powerful, too. No? That mystery alone can be a reason to attend. One meeting won't hurt. Who knows, it could also be the funniest thing I've seen in years, or in my case, ever.

***

To keep busy, I roamed the streets of Mardi Town while handing out surveys. I might as well get invested to the maximum with my work. The project I'd put on the back burner for the office of tourism is what I can work on at the moment. With all properties booked for February, I have time. Time can be toxic if not spent well. And work is a healthier alternative to spending time with alcohol. I'd rather cope while making more money than falling into a hole I'd keep digging.

The surveys are for retrieving information from the people who live here and know better than anyone Mardi Town's charms. All about classic activities, must-visit places and must eat foods. When compiling the surveys, I'll create the most authentic data base of the town. Here comes my commission and advertising spot.

Hours passed. Frost formed on my boots, and my leather gloves lost to the glacial air. Though plenty of surveys had been completed, I wanted to stay longer. I was under the impression the cold affected my mind to the point it stopped thinking. And for me, that is a good thing. Troubles became nothingness and the void never felt so good. I want to stay here, walk on the crisp snow and smile at strangers. The small interactions gave me life. I'd be going too far, saying they made me feel alive. All went well until I smiled at the wrong person. That person was no stranger.

"Do you want to get sick?" Robert told me, his features creasing.

I put back the survey I was about to hand him in my folder.

"What do you mean? I'm working."

"I saw you outside an hour ago and the hour before that. Every customer in the café was busy filling out your survey. You must've given them to the entire town."

"I wasn't here long. Some people took many surveys and shared with others," I said, words escaping with difficulty from my frozen lips.

"Come, drink a coffee."

"I don't need it..." I mumbled.

He took away my folder and walked ahead, confident I'll follow. What can I do without my folder of surveys? Do impromptu interviews with cracked lips? I'm too cold to fight it off. If I stay longer, my body will go into hibernation. That's when you know you've gone too far.

I followed him, my shoulders reaching my ears and a trail of vapour leaking out of my mouth. My nose is clogged, hence my mouth has to do all the breathing.

After prolonged contact with the cold,

the warmth of the shop rushed through my body like fire. It had been hours since I could breathe a breath visible to none. While shivering, my eyes scanned the place for a spot. In mere seconds, an unconventional sight caught my eye.

Chapter 12

From my perspective, no matter when or where I see him, I feel it's unconventional. We're long past the time of his coffee break, yet here he is in the centre of the room, in his oversized black suit, at it again with his game of solitaire. I hurried to the counter where Robert poured steaming hot coffee into a white mug. In no circumstances should I give him the opportunity to notice me. Not that he'd spare me glances if I did. Neither would I. Not anymore. I'm done with the bargaining stages and the process of grief altogether.

"Thank you," I whispered to Robert,

warming my hands with the mug first.

"Why are you whispering?" Robert asked in a volume much louder than mine.

Then I realized how silly I acted. Why should I whisper or try to avoid his attention? I'm a regular too. The reason I'm here is obviously for the coffee, not him. I don't know who frequented the place first, but the intention's the only thing that matters.

"My voice is a little weak from the cold." I said to excuse my whispering.

"Drink up," he then told me.

The fact that sound travels is the only thing keeping me from ranting about him to Robert. On other thoughts, I don't think that's it. To see him made me realize important things and perhaps he's forgiven —in the sense he's out of mind. My trouble with him didn't change my life. What was there to begin with isn't gone. And what wasn't there isn't here either. The biggest blow is the deterioration of my friendship with Auburn—and consequently, Laine. That loss causes my emptiness. While Avel caused our fight, the deepest problems formed before I'd met the man. It was a matter of time till Auburn confessed. At times, her words had hidden messages and I'm guilty of having ignored them. I thought myself paranoid and brushed off the signs. It hurts to admit the branch would have fallen by itself. Avel was simply a bird that momentarily sat on the cracked branch. Plenty of birds in the sky. Any of these birds could have been the one. Even the wind could have broken it off.

On the list, his trouble is quite low. After the broken friendship, we have the Crystal Mask. He succeeded in inducing fear and hypnotizing me. Thanks to him, I need to attend a suspicious meeting and receive follow-up calls from the police. The meeting's a choice but a pretty scary one. I feel inclined to accept the invitation. Similar to a lead character in a horror movie, feeling inclined to open the closet door.

All that to say, the loan that's never once been mine is now the least of my troubles.

"The coffee's getting cold," Robert said, peeking at my filled to the brim cup of coffee.

"You're right, and re-heating coffee is a crime," I replied, quoting him. I agree that re-heated coffee isn't as good. It tastes like tomato juice.

He showed a satisfied nod.

Not wanting to miss out on the warmth, I chugged the coffee.

"I can make you another one, fresh and warm."

"No need. This is fine. Thank you."

I wonder if Avel overheard my voice. My back is facing him, therefore my voice is the only hint he has. I wonder if he'd given me a glance. I hate the man but I find the coincidence of meeting him at 5 pm funny. That to me gives every indication he has nothing better to do—says the one who truly has nothing better to do.

What if he is, in fact, a loner? Given his personality, I wouldn't be shocked. That's enough. I won't let my curiosity driven by human instincts go any further.

"Say Robert, would you need someone to manage a social media account promoting this place?" I ask him to no longer be the person that has nothing better to do.

He bent a brow. "You hate social media and so do I. What's going on with you?"

He attacks me relentlessly with facts. It wouldn't hurt him to include white lies in his vocabulary. That would help me greatly with my mission to pretend everything's fine.

"Nothing's going on." In contrast, I'm the undefeated champion of white lies.

"Do you need money? Is that why you're working so hard?"

He couldn't have been more wrong.

"I've never lacked money since the business started thriving. I just like the labour. Other than social media, do you have odd jobs for me? I want to get busy."

"I think you need to get busy. Something is definitely wrong," he said, glancing at me here and there while working. "Occupy yourself with this."

He handed me today's paper.

"Is it me or do they copy paste the headline these days?" I remark, noticing the same old 'The Crystal Mask strikes again!'. "Can't they be more creative?"

"This is not a matter to get creative with. You've seen the man, aren't afraid?"

"I'm not sure."

Robert frowned as he walked out the counter. He's not one to poke his nose into another's business, but he worries and he asks...Until I confess. There's so much to confess that I'd rather keep it in. I don't want to hear advice I won't agree with. I don't want to break off another relation. Only after I complained to Auburn did we see our roads didn't align. Robert, being far more mature, would be careful with his advice. Yet, I can't blame myself for wanting to play it safe.

I'd love to talk to someone who'll listen without saying much. Someone who'll acknowledge what I say without placing judgment. I'll be getting things off my chest without fearing the consequences. Writing a journal is a not-so-bad option. To forget what I wrote, I could rip and burn the pages.

I blame human instincts for I'm about to do. I spun on the bar stool to face Avel. His stare pierced the cards on his table. Stuck again? The more I see him, the more I suspect he's a simple man. A man who spends his days working, drinking espressos and playing round after round of solitaire. He might just be content with that life. He doesn't look the least pitiful. Nor does he appear lonely—on closer observation. Alone isn't necessarily lonely.

That being said, let's leave him alone once and for all, as we both wished. Who says I want to spend time with him? I'd rather be alone than with him. If the world were to perish and we were the sole survivors, I'd attempt to survive on my own.

I spun again, going back to the newspaper on the counter. The Crystal Mask apparently struck again. I hope the article's not about my encounter.

I let out a sigh when reading he'd stolen valuable paintings from the Dofflers' house. Horrible family. Most of their paintings were sold by people faithfully believing the saying *'finders seekers'*—even if stolen. If the Crystal Mask is some kind of hero—doubt it—I hope he'll get the paintings back to where they belong rather than re-selling them in the guise of charity.

Whenever I hear of him, I can't help but recall his crystal blue eyes. They almost didn't look real. It was the first time someone's eyes mesmerized me. Basically, his eyes haunt me more than anything else at the moment.

"Thank you for the coffee," a voice from behind uttered.

Automatically, I turned, though I knew whose voice it was.

When he stood, his gaze fell on me as mine did on him. That's when I noticed his eyes. For the second time, I am mesmerized by a pair of eyes. A ray of sunlight shone through the window, making his eyes golden. Were his eyes this pretty the entire time? Before, all I could think of when I saw him was: loan rejecting jerk.

Chapter 13

It's not quite midnight yet, just 11:55 pm. In the night's darkness, the streets came alive with a burst of colourful lights. That's Saturday for you in Mardi Town. People strolled towards the night market, accompanied by their loved ones. Light bulbs of all colours adorned every edifice. How odd to have a secret meeting when the whole town's out and about? Sure they won't come near an elementary school, but what if they do, by accident? The gathering itself is not illegal. Hopefully. But we are meeting to find a thief; to an extent, that could be dangerous. Although he hasn't physically hurt anyone, he might if we get too close to his tail. All that was to say I find the choice of day and place plain stupid. I'd love to meet the genius behind the idea.

I took my time getting out of my house to arrive at around midnight. I wouldn't want to arrive early or late on top of being the needle in the haystack.

With each step I took away from the festive lights, a growing sense of unease overcame me. School scared me during the day, now I see it's worst at night. So many windows but no light. You end up staring, thinking a ghost dressed in a white dress will appear in one of them. When roaming the sombre hallway, you'd think it a matter of time before you hear a siren-like chant. Of course, a gentle piece would accompany it played on the piano in the music room. You could even go as far as to imagine the skeletons in the science room coming to life and chasing you around the school. Obviously, I imagined nothing while walking. I am unafraid, or rather realistic.

Being inside the school, I thought I'd bump into at least one member, but no. I'm all by myself, skin filled with goosebumps. With the flashlight of my phone illuminating the way, I search for classroom 6-B. The only sound I can hear is the clacking of my own boots. The absence of sound should offer reassurance, but at the same time, it poses concern. Either the stereotype of rich people being late is real or... Worst-case scenario: they're all early. They're waiting for me while tapping their fingers on the table, disappointment written on their face.

A tap on my shoulder and I let out a scream, deafening my own ears. I pointed the flashlight behind me and waved it frantically.

"My eyes!" someone said, wrath in their tone.

Steadying the light away from their eyes, I saw a man that never ceases to surprise me. Both time and place are mind-boggling in this case.

"Avel, you were rich?"

"What kind of question is that?" he said, blinking a few times to recover from the blinding light.

"Sorry for the flash and the question. I'm only shocked to find you here. No matter how weird you are, I don't expect you to enjoy little promenades in elementary schools at midnight. You must've been invited, and I thought only victims or likely victims of the Crystal Mask were invited..."

I struggled to articulate my thoughts and stumbled over my words. He's a banker. What fortune could he have? Was he an undercover director who had his fun at the bank?

"I'm a plus one," he said.

"You can do that? Is this a meeting concerning a local issue or a masquerade ball? If it's the latter, I'm overly under-dressed. Heck, I don't have a mask."

"Are you done? I'll be late because of you."

"I'm done."

The curtains closed, and our little skit

ended. Well, mine. I opted to follow him, because he seemed to know where he was going. Frankly, I was clueless about who I'd meet, yet I thought it'd make sense to see whoever I saw. Despite the hard to digest sight, I'll admit, I'm glad there's someone I am familiar with at this meeting. We might not be on good terms, but we are on terms if nothing else. Surrounded by strangers looking down on me, I won't feel alone. They'll look down on both of us. For a night, we'll be lambs walking into the lion's den. After taking a look at Avel, I realize my mistake. I'm sure even in a crowd of millionaires, he wouldn't turn into a lamb. He has a certain force, no doubt. His bottom lip is thick and relaxed. His eyes are sharp and always ready to cut. I'm not sure why I'm giving him compliments. Maybe It's a backhanded compliment. A way to express how cold-blooded I think he is. Or I genuinely think good of him now.

"Walk faster," he said, confirming that it was a backhanded compliment. No more, no less.

Walking faster, we finally arrived in front of the dreaded classroom 6-B. Curiosity and excitement brought me here until fear took their place in a jiff. Reality greatly differs from fantasies. The thrill of a secret society is long gone. Avel, on the other hand, is his usual stony self. There are no changes whatsoever in his expression or posture.

"Avel!" someone called.

We both turned around to see who it was.

"Fancy seeing you here," he added, talking to me this time.

Now what is a police officer doing here? Wasn't the letter criticizing the force and suggested we do their job? Is he the rat?

"You wrote my report and you think it's fancy seeing me here?" I said.

He looked at me, his eyes creasing into a smile.

"You know each other?" Avel spoke, evidently puzzled.

"We've met twice," the officer replied.

"At the club and the police station," I

added.

"The club? You're still going there in disguise, Ace?" then said Avel.

"Nothing wrong with it," the officer.

"You two are friends?" I asked in my turn, pointing back and forth.

"Ah, yes. Pardon my late introduction. My name is Aciano, but many call me Ace," he said, elegance flowing out of his fluid movements. "And you are acquainted with Avel? It surprises me he knows someone other than me."

I laughed at how accurate my own thoughts had been.

"I won't say he's a stranger. We met at the bank and at a coffee shop. We played cards and kept seeing one another at the most random times."

The moment I'd said that, Aciano turned to Avel, wide eyed. "You played cards with someone? I can't believe it!"

"Yeah, yeah, neither can I," he said, pushing him into the classroom. I went along with them, that is until I saw the inside of that said classroom. It looked nothing like a place elementary students attended. Desks were brought together in the centre to form a larger surface. Chairs occupying people stood around the table. The people held flashlights under their chins; the shadows of their features expanding. What did I walk into? Was the invitation a ruse for me to join a cult?

"Avel! At last you're here!" a brunette that dressed young despite looking well into her 50s stood from her seat. "Sit with me," she patted the chair on her side. Surely he won't sit there. He'll ignore her. Cause that's the type of guy he is.

I turned to see his reaction and my heart dropped. He flashed her a smile and walked towards her to then settle right where she patted.

"She's the one who brought him as a plus one," Aciano said, next to me.

"I see."

It's understandable for him to sit there, then. But the smile. That's Avel from a parallel universe behaviour. In his defence, the smile looked fake. Too forced to be sincere. He did the crease of the eyes and the curve of the lips, but it was too creased, too curved.

The closest to a smile I got from him was a laugh. His eyes glimmered then.

Avel turned on his flashlight and joined the cult. I have no other choice but to join the so-said cult as well.

"Are you here as a plus one too, Aciano?"

"Yes. Unfortunately, I won't be able to sit beside you, Miss Mint," he answered with such politeness.

I liked the sound of 'Miss'. Sadly, it has to end.

"Please call me Rene."

"Then please call me Ace," he retorted, his knowing smile back on.

"Alright then, Ace," I nodded.

"Rene."

A few more invitees entered the classroom and settled into a seat. I'd found a place next to a woman wearing a synthetic feathered coat that mopped the floor. She faced me and nearly gave me a heart attack. Though I expected the expanded shadow, I couldn't help but jump a little.

"Did I scare you, darling?" she said, her voice dry like crisp fallen leaves.

"No, no, I'm fine," I said, turning on my flashlight.

"Odd this meeting, isn't it? The host—whose identity we don't know—doesn't seem to be here yet," she continued.

The woman looked rather uncomfortable, having to squeeze her voluptuous body into a chair designed for someone many times smaller than her. With a swift movement, she retrieved a card from the inner part of her coat and extended it towards me.

"I am Sophie Croque, owner of the Bleu Bird theatre. You can call me Madame Sophie."

Out of obligation, I handed her my card as well. It read *Rene Mint, CEO of Rene Mint CO.* Original, isn't it?

"Are you a fashion designer? Strange that I haven't heard of your brand. You must be starting out. How cute." She told me, her eyes in a line and lips pursing into a smile more artificial than the wrinkle-free skin on her face.

My name did sound like a fashion designer's. Behold, the S/F collection from Rene Mint is one step closer to your doorstep.

Mirroring her previous expression, I answered: "I am not a designer. Describing my work would take too long. Let's simply say I'm in the real estate business."

"Is that so?" She spoke like she chewed bubble gum; the sound of her sticky lip gloss transferred her missing wrinkles to my forehead. Unease dropped on me as I realize I'd indeed come to a very shady gathering. The moment I'd seen the flashlights or even the dark hallways, I should've taken the cue to run.

The sense of unease grew when I glanced at Avel. That woman had her hands—with long and bright red nails—on his shoulders. She rubbed them up and down. Her eyes were wide open as though she looked at a jewel and her lips edged to the side, showing a joker-like smile. If that's her definition of a seductive expression, then I understand why her ring finger is empty and she has to resort to seducing her employee.

Avel sat there like the strange lady playing with his shoulders didn't exist. His smile disappeared—no surprise there. A man like him couldn't maintain a smile for so long, even a fake one. Instead, he responded to every word she said, with sentences half the length of hers.

"What's on your mind, Avel?"

"Nothing much."

"I'm scared. What if I am the Crystal Mask's next victim? You know I live alone in a vast villa."

Her voice was so breathy. She spoke as if she'd ran out of air or was in a desert, thirsty for a drop of water.

"That's what this meeting is for," he answered.

"You know that man?" Madame Sophie said, nudging my arm.

"You could say that," I replied.

"Oh, men. Eternally disloyal. You're fine leaving him with that cougar, Louella?"

I wanted to laugh, but I knew I'd get misunderstood if I did.

"He's not mine. He's free to go wherever he wants."

Madame Sophie beside me cackled, bringing the attention of the two we stared down so diligently. They both looked in different places. The woman looked at the cackling Madame Sophie, and Avel caught my eyes. Behind the emptiness in his eyes, there was a flicker of hidden emotion that I couldn't quite grasp.

"I know there's something between you two," Madame Sophie whispered in my ear.

"There isn't," I said in a normal voice. I didn't feel compelled to whisper since, without context, my words signified little.

Just as I was on the verge of deciphering the concealed emotion in his eyes, an interruption came about. By that I meant that an abrupt silence fell in the room and all eyes were on the last person to enter the room. When all seats were filled, the total count was eleven people. None took the initiative of a host, turning the meeting perplexing. We looked at one another warily. Goosebumps took over my skin as I regret and regret.

Chapter 14

"What are we waiting for?" Louella said, her voice trailing off into the air.

Unlike the others, she didn't look around in confusion. Avel was the sole focus of her gaze. That made my blood boil. It's not about Avel sitting next to her, but her sitting next to him. This woman is using her status to take advantage. Oddly enough, I never thought Avel would be in such position. That doesn't seem to fit his character.

"We're waiting for the host, isn't it obvious, Louella?" said a man I know by the name of Emery Shaffer. He owns the biggest golf course in town—perhaps the only.

In a sea of familiar faces, she stood out as someone unknown to me, despite my knowledge of the powerful people of town.

"How impertinent, that host. Being late to their own gathering," the one who spoke this time was Emmett Moor. He's an unpopular politician. I've never agreed with him since his opinions are close-minded and his decisions, hypocrite.

"Maybe the host is already here," I said to stir up things.

I feel the weight of everyone's stare in the room and flinch without thinking.

"What do you mean by that and, by the way, who are you?" asked a person I recognized as Vance Blankship. He's the owner of the largest retirement home in Mardi Town. His gaze scanned me up and down as though the table didn't hide half my body.

I had planned to answer when someone beat me to it.

"I know who she is. She's the new money girl. You know, the one who arrived last year and is already raking in loads of money in town," said Dionne Van Riel, the undefeated pharmaceutics queen of town.

I've become familiar with these individuals through reading the news every day. To have never met them before was surely a blessing in disguise. The blessing's over though. I wish it were possible to turn back time and to have never read that letter.

"Ah, I've heard of her. Though, that money isn't much," Louella spoke up. She, at last, tore her gaze from Avel and focused on me; her lips pursed.

If she mattered, the news would've mentioned her.

"The term 'new money' doesn't even fit her," Louella said. "Yearly income wise, she hasn't reached the millions yet."

The entire group burst out laughing. They were in fits of laughter, holding onto their stomachs for support. I was ridiculed.

Yes, the money I make is the money they spend on their yachts's toiletries. All I want to say is that I'm growing. New money is either getting rich overnight or by growth. I'm the latter.

"Why is she even here? I had the impression this meeting was for the most likely victims. In simpler terms, those with considerable wealth."

I cleared my throat, knowing I had an explanation none could deny.

"First, my business is growing. It won't be long till I reach the millions. And who knows, maybe the billions too? And at last, I am not a likely victim. I am a victim. I caught the Crystal Mask in my apartment not too long ago. He ran away before he could steal a thing."

In response to the unexpected revelation, a mix of gasps and doubtful glances spread.

"You're lying. You made this up to be invited," Louella said, seemingly doubting me the most.

"How could I have known of this

meeting?" I replied. "The invitation was in my mailbox. I didn't buy it."

"She has a point," silently said a man in the back. This one too, I didn't recognize. He wore a black fedora hat, black sunglasses, and a black long coat. "Now's not the time to take it out on a newcomer. Aren't we here to find the Crystal Mask?"

His words sparked unity, and all nodded their heads. No one questioned the mysterious man. Only I was clueless.

"What he said is correct," another added. "It's likely that many of you are already familiar with me, but for those who aren't, let me introduce myself. I'm Jorge Moss, the former chief of police." Pointing to Ace, he added: "I've brought with me a man I have high hopes for. Despite my retirement, I remain well connected and able to provide assistance."

"What about the other youngster?" Madame Sophie remarked, pointing to Avel, who was the remaining youngster which none knew.

A sense of relief washed over me when

the burden of scrutiny lifted and shifted to another.

"Is he your new toy?" asked Dionne, the pharmaceutics queen. "You are aware that you're not supposed to bring your toys to work," she added, her lips red apple and seductive.

"He's not a toy," she responded so lazily. It's as if she didn't mean it. "Avel is the most intelligent employee at the bank. I convinced him to come, considering we'd really need the help."

Common knowledge for rich people. Make the little people work for them. Why use your brain when you can pay someone to use theirs? Her brain must be rotten by now—that is to say it ever worked in the past.

"But is he trustworthy?" asked the former chief of the police.

He's the least suitable person to be questioning him. The man is going against the force he once pledged to be loyal to. To make matters worse, he brought along someone who is currently working for the police. If they were to be discovered, Ace would be in more trouble. I doubt his connections could save either of them then.

Avel falls under the same category. No matter how handsome Louella thinks he is, to save face, she'd throw him under the bus.

It isn't like me to pity people—of all kinds.

"He's the type of person who'd rather walk on his own lips than talk about others."

Her line was outdated and inaccurate. Surely they fed her that bank via silver spoon.

"Case closed then. We can start," Mr. Moss said with a clap.

"Without the host?" someone commented from the back.

"If I may say," Avel began—coming out of his cave. "The host might have already taken a seat and opted not to reveal their identity for precautions."

I had the same idea, but I didn't get the chance to voice it. They kept cutting me off and talked about my wealth as if I weren't in the room.

"I told you he's smart," Louella said, tapping his arm with eyes gleaming.

"All the more reason to begin," Mr. Moss repeated. "We, too, should be discreet in our investigation."

"Can't we hire someone?" the politician, Emmet Moore, said.

I expected nothing less from him—someone who sits on his butt all day and receives a paycheck for it.

"Why have the meeting then, Emmet?" Mr. Blankship said. Nobody in this room fancied each other; a cockroach passing by could tell. Their faces were tense, their brows furrowed and lips tightly pressed. It's unclear to me whether it was fear or an inflated sense of confidence.

We thoroughly talked about the Crystal Mask. Everyone shared what they knew and what the police had in their files. Merely hearing the information felt illegal. Is it? I didn't force anyone to reveal confidential information. They're speaking out of their own will.

What I've learned is that the Crystal Mask has a fixation with documents along with the obvious—expensive goods. He's been stealing business documents from every house he'd visited. Due to my contribution, they've figured out he seizes documents first. And that must mean something, because their faces dropped the moment they realized their businesses were also in danger. Who knows, the goods might only be phase one of his plan. That could also have been a distraction to make them loosen their guards thinking that was the end of it. Of course, I didn't share my theory because that would ruin the fun.

"He's one person. How much damage could he do?" asked Louella, her eyes care free. She didn't seem to be as worried as the rest.

"He's done enough to show how much one person can do," Madame Sophie said.

Afterwards, we discussed the money he stole and how untraceable it was. Ace explained that part since he had been part of the hunt.

"He didn't leave a trail. He sent money here and there anonymously. The money was scattered in various amounts and mixed with the other donations. Without exact proof, we couldn't claim the money from the organisations."

The next topic was the fascinating mask he wore. All attention was on me when I explained the sight I'd seen that night.

"The crystals shone brighter than any jewel you might own, I'm sure. That mask is honestly the worst costume for a thief. He got caught because I heard the crystals hitting one another while dangling down his face. I think we should investigate that mask. That might also be a stolen item; a very expensive one at that. We might find a lead by looking at its origin."

That mask might be his origin story. A story to be told for generations.

"Let's assign our partners and call it a night. I'm way past my bedtime and my skin won't be too happy about that," said Dionne Van Riel, the pharma queen, breaking the nerve-wracking atmosphere I managed to build up.

"Yes, my wife will start to worry if I'm not home soon," continued Mr. Shaffer, the golf centre man.

One by one, they nodded.

"We can choose our partners, right?" Louella said, her arms glued to Avel.

I saw the glint in his eyes. He silently pleads for help. Those eyes say 'save me from my misery.'

I find myself conflicted. On one hand, I'd love to see him suffer. An effortless revenge is what I'd call it. And on the other hand, I could not see Louella get her ways. Were she nicer during the meeting, I wouldn't blink an eye at Avel's unspoken request.

"I propose we do it at random. Does anyone have a deck of cards?" I ask eyeing Avel. "We'll need eleven cards. Each will have its pair for the exception of one who'll have an additional identical card. We're an odd number, thus we'll have duos and a trio."

The host did write to be creative when picking teammates.

"It all sounds good, but who would carry a deck of cards on them?" Mr. Moore said, hiding a snicker.

Before they could laugh—again—Avel stood, taking out of his pocket a deck of cards. I am thankful for this man's addiction to cards and regret to have doubted him for even a second.

"He's always well prepared," said Louella, showing off her teeth implants. She wants to brag but can't help but be nervous about the fact they may not be partnered.

Avel handed me the deck without a glance and I picked out the cards I needed without hesitation. Four different pairs and one trio. I won't cheat, since me not wanting Louella to get her ways is not me wanting to be partnered with Avel. Actually, I'd love for fate to link me with Mr. Pacheco, the man wearing all black from head to toe. Madame Sophie had told me of his name and of his work. All she knows is that he owns multiple businesses and gets richer by the second. Even now, as he breathes, money enters his pockets from various—unknown—sources.

If we were partners, he would no longer be so mysterious. I could even ask him to take me under his wing. Then I'll become the richest of them all. These good-for-nothings will beg for an invite to my tea time.

"You can turn your card now," I said after having handed everyone a card.

It's time to look at what fate has in store for me. Turning my card, I saw my stalker. That card stuck to me like gum. The three of diamonds faced me anew. That card is ironically—intentionally—the one of our sole trio. Was it not enough that I had to be paired with one of these people I need to be with two of them? Let's hope Mr. Pacheco is one of them.

I snooped around to see who I was matched with. Madame Sophie had a five of clubs and was very unhappy to have matched with Mr. Blankship. You couldn't deny that at least it's a convenient match. Her theatre is next to his retirement house.

With twinkling eyes, I observed Mr. Pacheco, and they dropped when soon enough he shook hands with Mr. Moore.

Mr. Moss, the ex chief of police, matched with Ms. Riel.

Five people remained. Mr. Shaefer, Louella...Ace and Avel. Louella turned the card painfully slow. A nine of spades, thank the stars!

Not so soon...

"You're with us, Rene," Avel said, making Louella turn her head.

"You two know each other?" she asked, the world crumbling before her eyes.

"We're rummy buddies," I said, crushing the debris on my way.

"What buddies now?" she said, glaring.

"You know, the card game?"

Realization probably hit her when she eyed the deck belonging to Avel.

"Louella, we're partners," Mr. Shaefer said, taking her away.

When I turned to my team, Ace was all

smile and Avel, all quiet.

"Happy to be working with you, partner," Ace said, reaching out a hand.

"Same here," I said, gladly taking his hand. I have a good hunch about Ace. "What about you, Avel? Aren't you happy to be working with us?"

He scoffed. "What makes you think I'm even happy to be here?"

"I don't think of how you feel at all," I replied.

"Let's keep it that way."

"It's an improvement," Ace said. "Aside from me, Avel doesn't respond to anyone with emotion."

"How was that speaking with emotion?" Avel said.

"Is that so?" I said, grinning at Avel, who avoided my eyes at all cost. I'm curious to see how his face would change if we were to match eyes.

"Don't forget your mission everybody, and don't be obvious. That would defy the purpose of micro teams. Only share information with your partners outside of the meeting room," said Mr. Moor. He's acting like quite the host. Perchance, is he? Might be the leadership in him kicking in after a long time.

The upcoming days have the potential to be rather interesting. Ace won't be too bad and Avel will start to become tolerable —to say the least.

"I'll contact you both when it's time to investigate," Ace told us.

"I'll give you my number, then," I said.

"No need. I already have it."

"How?"

"You left it when you came by the station."

"You are a very shady police officer, you know? You're attending the meeting, divulged confidential information, and you're going through reports for your own gain."

I wouldn't be surprised to know he's the rat that shared my incident with the host. Or... Is he the host?

I looked at him full of suspicion while he stood there smiling like a fool.

Chapter 15

I've been told that I'm pretty when I cry. Then again, I've only heard it from the ones who've made me cry. Ever since, I felt the prettiest when shedding tears. And as I read a not-so mysterious letter, I know I'm drop-dead gorgeous.

What a bad idea to have gone outside with the letter. If anyone asks, I'll blame the wind.

The letter goes in the nearest garbage. But that doesn't change a thing. They know where I am and who I am now. Simply changing everything wasn't enough.

Would they even find me if I launched

myself to the moon? *Probably.*

Now that I've received this letter, I realize it's only a matter of time before someone from my past emerges. But, my plate is full and I couldn't care less. While my beginning might have been an escape, I've later learned to live for myself. I'm no longer hiding, I'm living. Nobody fed me this life. I crafted it. Therefore, no one can snatch it from me. I promise to myself that this is the last time the past wells tears in my eyes.

With that, I flick my lighter on and bring it to the cigarette hanging out of my mouth. Having not smoked in a while, I take a harsh inhale, the earthy taste of tobacco exhilarating me. Wouldn't it be alright to smoke just one? I would've nearly collapsed if I hadn't.

I've gotten stranger. My hand tingles at the sight of a couple holding hands. As I walk past them, I get a glimpse of their faces. Not a single concern clouded their eyes. They look so peaceful it's utopic. My deepest desire is reflected in them, like a mirror. A mere cigarette won't do the trick. As I come to my senses, I flick it in the garbage. No good will come out of smoking.

***

"I tried to search online for the crystal mask I saw, but all that came up was news of the Crystal Mask and cheap masks sold for costume purposes," I said, picking up another card.

"The mask is a dead end," Avel told me, reaching for the card I'd laid on the table.

"No, no. There is something about that mask. I'm telling you."

In the guise of sharing progress on our investigation, Avel and I met up for coffee. After all, what's suspicious about two people playing cards at a café? Our conversation may be questionable, but no worries, we sat at the far end of the place. No one likes to sit there since it's a darker spot, far from any window. Robert isn't interested in filling the ceiling with light bulbs. He brought us a lantern, though, for our cards to be visible.

Despite our placement, we quieted down when it came to sensitive information. Ace isn't here because he finds this meeting risky. He is a police officer and meeting in broad daylight would... Would it really be fishy? As long as no one hears, they'll think he's meeting friends, and isn't he? Avel and he are friends. He and I are friends. Avel and I are... Acquaintances!

"What about you? What do you have?" I ask Avel.

"I had Ace send me the list of all the robbed houses and tried to find what they had in common."

"Did you need a list to find out he goes for the rich? Just tell me you did nothing. I'll understand."

Avel didn't flinch or show any sign of annoyance. Instead, he calmly responded: "It's not all they have in common. The Crystal Mask isn't lumping the same eggs in a basket."

"Meaning?"

"Meaning the rich households that were stolen from had shady business ethics in common. That's why he looked at the papers first. For proof they're scums."

A man of few words, and for once, true words. His explanation makes perfect sense. A wave of relief hits when I realize I'm safe. The Crystal Mask hasn't visited again because he knows my business is genuine. I'm off the list. I've caused no harm and stole no money. My account is filled with rightfully earned money.

"I guess those blue eyes of his are good," I said.

"Did you say blue?" Avel said, drawing back.

"I think they're contacts, though. Eyes can never be this blue."

"Why didn't you say so at the meeting? Every detail counts."

"I don't trust them," I say, frowning when I recall the dark classroom filled with people holding flashlights.

"And you trust me?"

"I haven't thought of that," I say, taking a step back—in my mind.

"You can trust me," he says and I cannot not look at his face. "I side with no one and work for none," he continued.

Not what I expected.

"You sure like to contradict yourself," I say, shifting back my gaze to what mattered more, the cards.

"Care to explain?" He leaned forward, and all I saw were strings on his back being pulled by Louella from afar.

She had complete control over him last night. I won't say a thing, as there's no need for a misunderstanding.

"It's nothing."

"It's not nothing, it's slander," he said, not pulling back.

"Get back to the game and prepare for defeat."

"Like hell I am."

Avel must be quite competitive because he gave up on the subject and truly got back in the game, his pupils moving from card to card.

At the same time, my phone vibrated on the table and a message notification popped up.

Aciano: How's the secret meeting with your partner going?

Did he send me the message by accident? Did he mean to send it to his friend Avel? I still replied.

Me: Avel is being weird.

Aciano: Normal then?

Maybe the message was for me. I guess I've made a new friend. Nice.

"Ahem."

I've been on my phone and failed to notice Avel was waiting for me to play my turn.

"I'm working," I said, briefly showing my screen. "I'm discussing a grave matter with our partner that couldn't join us."

"It's not that he couldn't, he didn't. He's being dramatic. Let him be."

Me: Avel says you're dramatic.

I've never thought of Avel as dramatic until he muttered the term. It fits him like a glove. So the saying's right, birds of a feather do flock together.

Aciano: Says the one who taught me how to.

Like I said.

I wasn't able to hide the grin that caused Avel to give me a death stare. The grin grew larger because of his stare. Why do I find it funny suddenly?

The phone rang and looking over, I'm disappointed it's not Ace. I thought he'd call offended by Avel's antics.

"Don't answer the phone. He's the type to never hang up."

"It's not him, it's the cleaning agency," I say, picking up the phone. "Hello?"

"Ms. Mint," the voice of the man carried tenseness, "I'm calling because there's been an incident."

"What kind of incident? Please tell me what's wrong?" I said.

Taking a peek at Avel, it's evident the call piqued his interest.

"I came to clean the apartment on Cherry street and was very shocked to see its state."

"Tell me calmly," I say, expecting nothing. I find it helps soften the blow.

"The place is a complete mess. I can't describe it. You'll need to see for yourself."

"I'll be right there. Thank you for the call."

I might have sounded composed but there's nothing calm about me now. Out of all the troubles I still had to go through, it just had to be one that hits my business directly. My only pride. What I hold the dearest. Without it, I'm nothing. My work defines me. It's what awakes me in the morning and gives my day purpose.

"Is something wrong?" he asked.

"I have to leave. Apparently, one of my apartments was trashed, and I need to assess the situation before word gets to the landlord."

I huffed and puffed to put on my coat and the strap of my bag.

"I'm tagging along," he then said, gathering the cards.

I froze. "Why would you?"

"It could be the Crystal Mask's doing. I'm merely going to investigate."

Like I'll believe that. Not only is he dramatic, but he also has Pinocchio tendencies.

"Alright then. Tag along, Sherlock."

For some unknown reason, fear is starting to fade and what I'll see may be bearable.

Chapter 16

Somehow, I spent five minutes staring at a keyhole. The key's in my hand, but that's all there is. A key component—courage—is missing. Taking a step back, I bump into Avel, who's been behind me this whole time.

"Sorry," I said, a bit out of my mind.

He hadn't complained or released a sigh in the last five minutes. As though he understood how nervous I was, Avel stood silent. Didn't know he could be *considerate*. That's added to my list of things I ignored about Avel.

Fearing the end of Avel's consideration,

I resolved to finally unlocking the door. As I twist the knob open, I hope for this to be a prank. A joke coming from the boredom of an employee and in there is a freshly cleaned apartment. I'd ask for nothing more.

Asking was a waste of time.

A gasp escapes my lips as I am confronted with the sight. It's far worse than the images that've gone through my head on the way here. The place is unrecognizable. There are rips in the sofa, and its stuffing is all over the floor. That floor is marred by a puzzling black powder. The walls were vandalized with red spray paint. Kitchen stools were split in two and thrown around. The flat screen is cracked in the middle. My precious coffee tables I bought from an antique store were sloppily painted in various colours. This was an intentional job, and I'd be a fool to think otherwise.

"I don't even want to see the other rooms," I say.

I am devastated, to say the least.

"I don't think it's the work of the Crystal Mask," Avel said, stating the obvious. The Crystal Mask isn't a vandal, he's a thief.

"I've got nothing to fear, then."

"You've got everything to fear," he says grimly, the creases of his eyelids reaching his furrowed brows.

"I don't understand, though. Who and why?"

"Do you have enemies?" he asks.

Do I? I did meet the most influential people of Mardi Town most recently and the meeting wasn't...favourable. However, did I do something aggravating? Something that requires a retaliation of this scale? Most probably not.

Therefore, I answer: "No."

"Are you sure?"

"Do you think I'm the type of person that's bound to have enemies? Be honest."

"Successful people are bound to have enemies," he said, softening the blow.

That might be the nicest thing he's told me. I can't say a word after that and neither can he, I suspect. I brought my gaze elsewhere out of embarrassment. When they landed on the gutted sofa, reality brought me back.

"Enemies or not. I can fix this. It'll cost me, but I'll get this place running again in no time," I say, rolling up my sleeves—even though I will do no labour yet.

"I suppose Ace and I could help. We could use the place to have private meetings in the meantime."

What's gotten into him? In the mix of strangely caring words, Avel is trying to hold on tight to his image of a heartless jerk with his see-through excuses. Too bad he's blown his cover. I don't believe him anymore. If I continue to read between the lines, I might keep discovering some good in him. Though, I'm not sure what I'll do with that. Will that change a thing?

Suddenly, my phone buzzed and jolted me out of my thoughts. I wished for it to be another text from Ace. Those were funny. They weren't bad news. Looking at my phone, I understand that wishes coming true are fantasy. My knees gave out when I read the message. I live under a constant stream of surprises. Someone is going above and beyond to ensure I'm miserable.

"What's wrong again?" Avel said, kneeling next to me.

"My landlord said she saw the place. She said it's a strike."

The room is spinning, and the air is so heavy it's suffocating. This was supposed to be an easy fix. One where I'd only need to use money. Not even money can fix a strike. I'm doomed. Though it's not the last strike, it's pretty traumatizing. It marks the commencement of a countdown. If I were to lose this place, I could look for another, but word goes around. Landlords will be warned. What if they put me on a list? The process of finding a place will just be that much more troublesome. It may not be my fault, but it's my responsibility and well beyond my control.

"We'll remove the strike," Avel said, as if he'd heard my worry ridden thoughts.

I stare at his eyes and notice they're not

clouded anymore. No, when he speaks soothing words, they're honeyed.

"How can we do that?" I ask in a small voice.

"There's nothing you could have done to prevent this. We'll investigate, file a report, and show our progress to the landlord."

He kept mentioning 'we' and 'us'. A little bird—named Ace—informed me that's out of character of him. Despite how odd I think it is, I'm glad a composed person is by my side. He sees the situation objectively rather than emotionally. I had reached a point where I could imagine the future that lies ahead. It was nothing but my downfall. Avel wiped that imaginary future in the matter of seconds. I found solace in his words. How odd of him and odder of me.

I'm starting to realize that there's no harm in accepting help. Receiving support from others wouldn't mean I'm no longer an independent businesswoman.

I never dreamed that support would come from Avel, of all people. This man is a mystery, one I didn't know I'd feel like solving.

"I'll evaluate the damage in the other rooms. You stay here," he said, rising to his feet.

I stared in awe, thinking whether he was the same man I'd been bickering with over a round of rummy less than thirty minutes ago, or an alien that took over?

I stood up too, and only now felt embarrassed to have dropped to the ground. There was nowhere else to sit. Everything's broken or covered by fresh paint. How miserable.

Since Avel's assessing the other rooms, that leaves me with the kitchen. It appeared untouched from the outside until it reminded me that appearances can be deceiving. When I opened the cupboards, I saw that all the glasses were cracked, yet not broken. A single crack has the potential to render the cup useless, as tiny shards of glass can mix with the drink. The mugs had lost their handles, and the cutlery in the drawer was bent. The kitchen alone shows this act was driven by an act of revenge soaked in pettiness. No immature prankster would go this far. Strong intentions fill the place. I can sense it.

The real question is, who would despise me enough to commit to such destruction? Auburn and I had an argument, but I know she wouldn't sink to this level. The worst she'll do is ignore me. Despite the letter of this morning, I feel there's no speck of chance for it to be someone from my past. No one I can think of would be capable of this mess.

I think misfortune came knocking at my door by mistake.

***

While the elevator is going up, my mind goes down. I'm making a mistake. This is my last resort. It started out as a passing thought. Each time, I let it wander—never thinking it'd stay so close by. I blame the many happenings in my life for bringing me to this point. To the only immediate resolution. The one that ignores values such as patience and acceptance.

Someone pull me away before I go through with this.

The numbers on the screen above the doors are rapidly climbing. My hands are moist and my throat dry; I'm on the verge of a panic attack.

Should I? Should I not? There's no flower to pick out petals from for an answer. The bell rang, and the doors opened. I stuck a foot in so that I can take my time. Time won't make a difference. My mind should have been made before walking to this building or entering the elevator.

I stepped out, understanding I'd disturb other people by reigning over the elevator. My legs paced around the hallway, back and forth—to think. You see, I've come to the office of a notorious loan shark. None would give me a million except for this one. My loan is always pre-approved here. But it's a given I won't taste profit for years since the interest rate will nearly make pay the house twice. It'll take years to scratch the surface of the loan and more years to become a millionaire. On the other hand, the stress of receiving strikes will vanish. With a risk comes a candy. Is the candy worth the ordeal? Having said that, it appears wiser to bear a year of stress to then plunge into eternal sweetness. Nothing's certain, really. At the end of the year, I could either be lying on the ruins of my business or bathing in its ever-growing success. Destiny has alternative endings.

Chapter 17

"Why is this the only place for us to meet?" Avel said, sipping on his brandy.

"I find it to be a great meeting place," I replied, appreciating the jazz playing inside.

"It's good to know someone understands me," Ace spoke through his second identity —the one with bleached white hair and edgy clothes.

"It'd be more suspicious to find us here than at the coffee shop," Avel said.

"This bar is ghosted. Do you see someone other than us?" Ace fought back with.

Indeed. The booths with red velvet sofas were all empty in the dimly lit place. The lack of people somehow gave off an eerie feeling. Were it not for the Jazz playing in the background, I would've questioned Ace's choice too.

"Why is it so empty?" I ask.

"I'm not sure myself. This speakeasy used to be popular."

"It's outdated," Avel said, shattering the romanticism of the place.

"You're outdated, Avel," I then told him out of spite.

He didn't respond and looked away. He must've not sensed the need to.

Ace laughed his head off before he realized we weren't laughing with him.

"Well, well, what have you two been up to in my absence?" he said.

It's my turn to look away now. I held gaze to the light bulb placed in the middle of our table. It sat on a wooden block and was much larger than regular bulbs. The light inside was dim enough to stare and not fear I'd lose sight.

"Do you have something to bring to the table, Ace? If not, I don't see the point in this meeting," Avel said, his tone cold as it was in our first meeting.

It may have been a mistake to believe I'd found good qualities in Avel the other day. Really, this might just be Avel. One minute he's nice, the other he's back. In my apartment, he's been nice for longer than a minute. It's possible that was just a lucky occurrence. If that's the case, I've used up all my luck with him.

"Why don't you two tell me first what you discussed at the coffee shop?" Ace persisted.

"We discussed little," I say. "I'm still looking into the mask and Avel found there's a possibility the Crystal Mask only targets owners of shady businesses."

If we were to send our little discoveries to the press, the public would surely make their mind. They'll call him a hero for doing the job the police hadn't succeeded on. He'll officially be Mardi Town's vigilante. I can only wonder why it took a vigilante to uncover these corrupt businesses?

I continued, "It's possible he won't stop at stealing and expose most of these rich people. Exposing them will leave more than a dent in their wallets. That blow would be hard to recover from. Despite their money and connections, it won't be easy to strike a deal with the Crystal Mask, as I suppose he wants nothing from them if he doesn't even keep the money. And maybe we should keep this theory between us..."

They both attentively listened while nodding their heads at the appropriate times.

"And why should we not share this prospect?" Ace asked, his tone phony as if it were a test.

"I don't agree with the Crystal Mask's ways, that's for sure. Yet, I don't agree with our member's methods either. Am I wrong for this?" I answer, unsure if it's satisfactory.

For a second there, I remembered Ace is

a police officer—despite his participation in the secret meeting, his authority can't be ignored.

"No, I think omitting these findings is a safe choice," Avel said, switching again. He seemed to be less irritated, his back settling onto the velvet couch.

"What about you, Ace? How far are you in the investigation? Compared to us, it is your day job," I say.

"Well..."

He's got nothing.

"Let's leave then," Avel added.

"No, wait!" Ace flailed his hands around, trying to keep us seated. "Rather than taking importance in information, we should take action is what I was trying to say. Take proper measures."

Avel, who was about to stand, took his seat back and raised a hand for a re-fill of his brandy. I too needed a refill of my whisky.

"I was thinking we could try to predict his next target and catch him in the act," he continued.

"Shouldn't this be done by the police?" I remark. "Rectification, shouldn't this have been done by the police?" I added, knowing I was talking to an officer.

"Many laws prevented us from it. We need permission to do a stakeout in someone's home, but as if they had a lot to hide, none agreed," he said, lowering his head. "Since we're now on the same side, perhaps we could get their consent...is what I thought. I might be wrong."

This appears to be the reason Ace accepted to take part in these ridiculous secret meetings. He's a driven man with only the thought of catching this criminal on his mind. He can't be biased by the public's opinion. To find him, he stooped to his level of outlaw. Because that's what the Crystal Mask is, an outlaw.

"How do you plan on finding the—" I zipped my mouth when I saw the server Avel called approach our table.

"Another brandy," Avel says.

"Another whisky, please." I say.

"A draft beer for me. Thanks," Ace

finished the order with.

After making sure the server was back at his counter where it's too far to hear, I proceeded.

"How do you plan on finding the next target?"

"We do have a list of potential victims."

"Are you going to let a pendant hang until it stops on a name?" Avel then said.

His flat tone made it impossible for us to laugh as though it wasn't meant to be a joke. We grew quiet, having nothing better to say.

The server had come by and handed us our drinks while our table remained soundless. I'm sure we're all thinking about how to crack the Crystal Mask's formula.

How could we possibly find the next target when the list—I can assume—is pages long? If ever he himself chooses a name on his list at random, our only hope is luck. Problem is, luck can be unreliable. There is little to no chance we guess right.

"We'd increase our chances if we picked three targets and do our stakeouts separately," I then say.

"I'm not sure it's a good idea for you to stake out on your own. If you meet him again, there's no saying what he'll do to you," Ace said, his eyes creasing apologetically.

I looked over at Avel, who nodded at Ace's caution.

"He didn't seem to be the violent type. I know him more than you two. Must I remind you we talked? Well, I talked, and he listened."

"Appearances can be deceptive. Aren't you old enough to know that?" Avel said, crossing his arms.

It pains me to not have a comeback in mind. My sole option is to explain.

"It's intuition rather than a judgment based on looks. Besides, I couldn't even see him when that mask was covering everything."

I guess that shut him up because any smugness he had left disappeared from his face

"Intuition is not very scientific," Ace

said.

This little meeting of ours gives every sign of being futile. The whisky's good, the company I would say is bearable, and the conversation's mediocre. Are we by any chance, enjoying the meeting, regardless of how unnecessary it is? The company might be a little more than bearable. Bearable with ease.

It's a given that when I start to get comfortable or settled, something has to happen. Here, it's a phone call from Auburn. I stare at my vibrating phone, my finger on the side, ready to silence it any minute now. I didn't. For the sake of the hope I secretly carried, I excused myself from the booth and took the call in the alley outside the speakeasy.

"Hello," I said, my tone like granite.

"Rene," she carefully muttered, her voice a pitch higher. "Could we talk?"

"Could we?" I scoffed.

Just when I realized I was better off alone, she calls me and shakes up my newly formed opinion towards friendship.

"Do you have time?" she says.

"I am in the middle of something."

"Come to my house after you're done. I need to talk to you."

The audacity she has to tell me to visit her house when it's already dark out and I'm not sure when I'll be done here.

How stupid I am to have accepted.

Satisfied, she hung up, and I can't seem to lower the phone. A call so objectively short felt subjectively long. The mere seconds I considered accepting were painfully extended in my brain. Auburn had hurt me a lot. Her words were needles that hit scars instead of a blank canvas. It happened in its full glory and I can never pretend I'm fine. That it's forgivable. Hence, I think an ordinary apology won't cut it. When I accepted to talk, I built the expectation that she'll be creative and genuine. That she'll cite everything she was wrong about. And that she'll remind me of how much she loves me. If she ends up going below my expectations, then I'll know it's time to cut off the link for good.

I'm not so sure I even want her to go beyond my expectations. I'm not sure anything in the world could erase what happened between us. What she said and what she thought. My mind goes back and forth. All I wish for is that it settles.

Back to the speakeasy, I catch Avel and Ace sharing a few words. Now I'm not liking the idea of having to be somewhere after. I want to see where the night will lead us.

Chapter 18

We'd talked of everything other than the Crystal Mask for the rest of our gathering. The subject seemed to have gone over our heads. Our last topic had been valentine's day because it was tomorrow. That day's the only thing Avel and I can agree on. We both despised the commercialized and outdated folk tradition. Ace was left out when saying he loved the idea of a day dedicated to love, even though he had no one to share it with. Avel called him stupid, and I continued by saying I no longer had faith in love. Anything regarding love made me sick, I told them. Ace tried to convince me I was malfunctioning. That there was a bug in my system while Avel reassured me by stating I was right for a change.

After that heated debate, we played cards since Avel carries a deck everywhere he goes. What a weirdo.

We called it a night after a few rounds. The day had already been so eventful. For Avel and me, this was our second meeting. Further, let's not forget the incident at my apartment. Lost in our game, I barely thought of my first strike and the ravaged apartment. Of course, as soon as we separated, the worries rushed back. The thought of Auburn's call reminded me that my day was far from being done. Lucky Avel and Ace, who can go straight to their homes.

I considered bailing. To tell her I was too tired tonight—that wouldn't be a lie. I even thought of leaving her hanging all night with no news. Maybe then she'll experience a fraction of my pain.

A few minutes later, I found myself in

front of her door. Despite the creative options, I settled for the original. I had the feeling this is a do or die situation. If I delay the talk, there might never be one.

Once I rang the doorbell, it was too late to flee. While her footsteps neared the door, I prepared mentally. I kept repeating in my head, *let's get this over with*—not knowing what I truly desired. Did I come here wanting to accept her apology or to end it once and for all?

"Rene!" she exclaimed, opening the door.

Her eyes opened like clams and her lips... I never knew they could stretch that much.

She wore the same nightgown she'd worn during a sleepover the three of us has at my place a few months ago. The satin gown is scarlet red with laced shoulder straps.

"Come in, come in!" she says, and to me everything is suddenly suspicious.

I had never fought with Auburn before, making this case unprecedented. Despite the unfamiliarity, I can tell this is out of the ordinary for Auburn. Whether this is a good thing is uncertain.

"I prepared snacks," she told me, pointing to the plate of store-bought Italian cookies on her coffee table. I recognized them since I buy the same. We both had no patience for baking.

The cookies may be part of her strategy. If this fight were petty and innocent, the soft cookies with dark chocolate cream would have contributed to our reconciliation. Now, I'm insulted by the idea. With a fight of this scale, it's even remarkable I accepted to hear her out.

"I have things to tell you," she says, her hands neatly placed on her knees.

Her stretched features had toned down, and the air of the room had turned more solemn. Now, she almost appears uneasy.

I, for one, will not say a thing unless I feel called to. It'd be a waste of energy to fight, as well as false hope for her. I accepted with expectations, but I'm exhausted. Could it be that the ship has already sailed?

A strained silence fell over us when I sat without a word. My act is adding oil to the fire, I know. In my defence, she started the fire and provided the oil.

"So... I realize that I might have been a bit harsh the other day," she said, wincing.

The little words ruined the apology. 'I realize I've been harsh' would have sounded a tad more accurate. If she were accurate, she'd be on her knees begging or at least use larger words such as I was extremely harsh and wrong.

Still, I say nothing and let her continue —in fear we'd bicker at her every line.

"I want to make amends. I couldn't help saying what I said because I don't know enough about you. You never told me about your life before coming to Mardi Town."

Here we are to the part where the blame is shifted around. All that in a honeyed voice.

"Say something," she says. "Please, I don't like this fight."

"And I don't like your reasoning," I said,

knowing I could no longer avoid speaking.

Auburn appeared to be running out of words, granting it should be the opposite. You could take out a million excuses regardless of how pathetic they sound. You could repeatedly say sorry. Or say things such as, "I didn't mean it." "It was a mistake." "I'm sorry that I hurt you. I was stupid."

"I said I'm sorry," she said in a pout. "What can I do to change your mind?"

Understand that mind first.

Is what she knows of me insufficient? Does our time spent together matter little compared to my past? The blame falling on me is the last thing I expected on the way to her apartment. Surprises never cease to disappoint me this week.

"There's nothing you can do," I answered.

Auburn stood in a rush. "That's not fair. It's foul to not even give me a chance," she said, distress in her voice.

She's the victim, and I am the assailant now.

"You were the one to give the hurt and expect to resolve it with an insincere apology." I said, my energy drained.

All I crave is the comfort of my bed.

"Insincere? I poured out my soul and you brush that away with ease," she said, her words heavy with emotion.

My blood boiled when she claimed I wasn't being fair. Nothing is ever fair. To Hope for a different outcome when it came to friendship was just my pipe dream. What was my only safe place in this upside down world is no longer.

If she'd poured her soul when we first fought, she'd have realized and apologized on the spot. Then I'd forgiven her in a heartbeat. She blew the chance she thought was never given.

"It's not worth it, Auburn." This may be the very last time I say her name. "I'll go home now. Please forget about me. It seems I didn't know you enough, either."

I considered her a best friend for the reason I never had one. Our girl talk never was too intimate. It never reached the deepest crevices of the heart. I mistook her for a close friend because I don't know how it feels to be so close to someone.

Auburn is trying to return to the good old days, but those days are blurring. Cookies won't bring back the memories.

"Don't go, Rene," she says, holding on to my clothes as I walk to the door. "We can patch things."

To patch up things would be kicking dust under the carpet. How can I trust her again? How can a day go by without me wondering if she's pretending to like me? There were no possibilities in the first place and my visit was simply for closure.

"Let me go. I need to go home," I said as I started to experience homesickness.

I longed to be in my safe space, the one only I have access to—I suppose the Crystal Mask, too. My home could never betray me or hurt me. It's entirely mine.

It's possible that she understood this because she unclasped her fingers and released her grip. Without taking another look at her face, I left, gripping my own clothes with similar force.

* * *

In the comfort of my bed, I awake and welcome the sunshine seeping through my half opened curtains. I was too worn out to close them last night. That day was unforgettable, to say the least. While I wish to erase it from my memory, some moments leave me to hesitating about that wish.

I had nearly forgotten the date until the calendar on my bedside table gracefully showed me. The dreaded February 14, Valentine's day. No, this day is like any other. Solely the 14th and I should treat it so. No more, no less.

Just as I tried to get rid of my grogginess, the doorbell rang. I am nowhere near presentable. As if the alcohol I drank at the bar was meagre, I chose to empty my secret stash of whisky last night. You wouldn't need a secret stash when living alone, but when you have a friend like Laine, you must.

Had.

She didn't return the bottle she took last time, hence why I resorted to the secret stash. I suppose I no longer need to keep it a secret. The bottles can be next to the innocent water bottles in the fridge and no one will complain. My drunk self was ahead of time and left a trail of whisky bottles exposed on the floor of my bedroom.

I tied my tangled hair into a bun to somehow resemble a human rather than the ghost coming out of the TV in The Ring. And I tried my utmost best to drag my feet to the door. My head keeps dropping and tilting. I'm having trouble holding it upright. The hangover's going strong.

I placed my eye on the peephole and end up seeing no one. Not a head or a chest. Was the single minute I spent on my hair too long for the person who rang? Despite seeing *air,* I felt the need to open the door.

My senses are always right. What I couldn't see through the peephole appeared at my feet when opening the door. A basket full of flowers. I recognize the flowers. They're white tulips. Typically, they are sent as a gesture of apology, seeking to make amends. Auburn? If cookies didn't do the trick, flowers will absolutely not. A card stuck to the basket's handle. Before disposing of the basket, I think it's appropriate to verify my assumption.

I am deeply sorry for the intrusion. I've failed to recognize at first glance you weren't corrupted like the others. Pardon my grave mistake and rest assured that your home is safe. It will never happen again.

C.M.

With a swift motion, I brought the basket inside and closed the door. This is not a public matter—or is anything else concerning my life... But this. No one must know. C.M. can only be the Crystal Mask. And his message confirms Avel's theory. The documents he caught a glimpse of proved I wasn't a suitable target since I've broken no laws to earn my living. I can't believe a wanted criminal gave a better apology than someone I used to call my best friend. His words even brought me reassurance.

I am sure now that this theory needs to stay hidden from the members of our secret meetings. Expose them, Crystal Mask. Take out the garbage. There's no way I can convey those words to him. He is untraceable. The flower must have been delivered by someone else. Even if he'd come to my door himself, that wouldn't change a thing. Surely he'll be hidden in plain sight. Without the mask, I won't be able to recognize him. And going to every flower shop asking who bought white tulips will be pointless. If he's clever enough to bypass the police, I'll never be led to him with these measly ways.

Out into the hallway, I walk slightly further from my door. I'm trying to get a whiff of his perfume. That could indicate he's been here. With each step, I leaked with disappointment. There was no musk or woody notes.

When I heard someone open their door, I dashed to mine. Let's not forget how I look. I haven't had the chance to see a mirror, but I know to skip that chance today.

The thought of alcohol suddenly gave me an idea. I run to my room and grab the empty bottles of whisky. I rinse them a couple of times and fill them halfway with water. They'll be the vases to my tulips. After cutting the stems, I slip a few flowers into a bottle and a few more in another. Taking a step back, I see on my kitchen counter a line of tulips in whisky bottles. I'm glad to have seen the card and kept the flowers. But really, should I be glad? Rooting for the outlaw questions my morals and this world I live in.

Chapter 19

I don't look for signs. If it's meant to be, they'll find me themselves. The flowers came, and I indirectly made contact with him again. This time, he was the one to relay words while I couldn't. That ends our first conversation. I had asked him question, and he answered them a few days later with an apology and even a gift. The sensation we'll meet again is overpowering.

"What are you smiling about? Are the pictures on the wall that nice?" Robert said, bursting the day dreams where I reminisced.

"I like the music you're playing today."

"It's the same jazz instrumental every day. I haven't changed it once."

"I knew that, just wanted to show some appreciation."

I hadn't noticed that he never changed the shop's music. I guess I'm not very attentive to details.

"I didn't realize you could be peppy," he said, taking a seat behind the counter.

"I'm not peppy and never was," I said, giving the faintest pout.

"You've been busy these days. Wanna tell me what you've been up to?"

I've been unable to share anything with Robert lately. The last thing I told him was the visit of the Crystal Mask and that feels like it's been ages. Much more occurred after.

In Robert I can trust. Unlike with Auburn, there will never come the day where I think I've misjudged him. There's no doubt about that.

I put a hand over my mouth and whisper to him the details, "Well, I was invited to this meeting to find the Crystal Mask—"

"That stupid thing," he cut me off, "I got an invitation, too."

"You did!" Well, that's a plot twist. "I didn't see you there."

He rubbed the back of his neck. "You're telling me you attended?"

"Yes."

"Why?"

"I was curious."

"Curiosity killed the cat."

"I'm not a cat."

He clenched his jaw. "So what happened there?"

"Nothing much." I leaned forward to whisper the sensitive information, "We each have a partner, in my case partners, and we're supposed to investigate together until the next meeting."

"I'm glad I ignored the invitation. I don't do well in teams. Who are you partnered with?"

"Avel, you already know him, and a guy called Aciano, but we call him Ace." I hesitated, but ultimately trusted him enough to tell the truth. "He's a police officer," I coughed out.

"What else?" he said.

Robert hadn't batted an eyelash at what I said.

"From the meeting? Nothing else?"

"I meant what else happened to you? You're rarely here at lunchtime."

Right. At this time, I should be blabbing away in Auburn's office.

"I had a disagreement with Auburn and it won't be fixed."

"Bummer," he said. "I wasn't very familiar with Auburn, but I'm guessing you made the right choice."

Then dawned on me the fact Auburn never came to Java Haze. She said it wasn't her style of café. If we ever met for coffee, we'd meet at some modern-looking place of her choice.

"I'm not done," I then say. "Something else happened."

"Quite the eventful life you got there."

"I wish it wasn't."

"Go on."

"One of my apartments got fully wrecked. I received a strike and need to renovate the place. Then I have to find the culprit and also the Crystal mask and—" I am breathless. As I verbalize my concerns, I understood my life became insanity reincarnated.

"Stop for a minute," he said, at last showing a sign of concern, his fingers tapping on the counter. "I hope you changed the lock of your place."

"About that," I said, wearily.

"Rene," he calls my name, standing from the stool. How terrifying, yet endearing.

"It's not what you think. Yes, I didn't change the locks, but it's no longer necessary. I'm not the Crystal Mask's target anymore. We have a theory and he confirmed it," I say with enthusiasm.

"We don't play with safety, Rene."

"Listen to the rest, will ya? He only targets dishonest people; the ones that cheated their way up. He came to my house to check my business documents. Don't say this to anyone, but he sent me white tulips with a card, admitting his mistake and assured me he'll never come back to my house."

Robert remained silent. Seems he isn't convinced quite yet.

"It's suspicious," he then said. "You will still change your lock, at least for the criminal who wrecked your property. You might be another's target."

"Do I look like a dartboard? Why am I everyone's target?"

"I wish I could do something," he said, his shoulders hunching down after sitting down.

"No, no. Being Robert of Java Haze is enough. I consider this place my second home; I can only experience genuine happiness here. And don't worry, I think my troubles are over. There'll be no more, no less."

"What do you know?" he says, the grouchiness in his voice back.

"I'm in good company. My partners

aren't half-bad. They also offered to help with the renovations."

"I do hope so," he said, side-eying me. "Be careful out there."

Soon enough, he'd left the counter to serve customers who had just entered the shop.

While I did only say Avel and Ace were agreeable partners to appease Robert, I'm thinking perhaps they really are good partners. The part where they offered to help with the renovations wasn't a lie. Avel had been with me the moment I witnessed the wreck. He willingly went there. I didn't ask him to.

Does that mean he cares? Am I overconfident, or is he really being protective? To be frank, I don't exactly know what that feels like. Being cared for, or protected. In my younger years, people seldom showed me interest. I spent a lifetime in my little corner, shivering. I feared the words of most people. How could I not when all they've told me was 'you're not worth a thing'? As I grew accustomed to the words, I believed in them. You can imagine the time and efforts put into undoing that mindset. In fact, it's a work in progress.

Chapter 20

As the day went along, Avel proposed to meet at the *damaged* apartment after his shift. We'd start to work on it without Ace since he has crucial work on his hands. He is a police officer and my recent case has nothing to do with the Crystal Mask, therefore he can investigate in broad daylight. Prior to catching my daily coffee, I'd handed him a copy of the keys and photos of the wreck. Funny thing is, Avel even gave me permission to let me write his name as a witness in the report. Maybe I really do have fine partners.

My hands held together in front of me, I wait for Avel in front of the complex. I pace around only because I'm cold; I am definitely not nervous about facing him. Why would I? He's nothing but a man. He turned out to be kinder than I expected, but regardless, he is still a man. The man I once dated at my lowest made me drop beyond the pit hole. As a result, I've become prejudiced towards love. I recognize, though, that my environment didn't offer me the best conditions for a healthy relationship. With a low self-esteem, my judgment was blurred and my choices rushed. Makes me wonder if what I experienced was love? After moving here, my conditions improved while my perspective of love remained similar as I watched Auburn go through it. Can it be that I was too single-minded? Is love so broad it varies by the person?

My overthinking tendencies don't prevent me from noticing the tall figure approaching me. His black coat was fully open, each side dangling in the wind, exposing his oversized attire. I'm beginning to suspect he owns identical suits in a range of colours. Sometimes, simple's best. And does his coat not come with buttons or a zipper too? The air's much too cold for an open coat.

"You're here early," he said and that could be his way of saying: 'I hope I didn't make you wait long'. Of course, that could also be my delusion.

"It hasn't been long since I arrived." I lied. "Let's go up."

We enter the warm building and head to the elevator. All of that in total silence. There's no basic conversation starter with Avel. He's anti-social and I'm not interested.

When the doors of the elevator closed, it dawned on me that I was in a tiny space with none other than Avel Malt. I never was claustrophobic, but it's creeping on me. I can't bear to look at his stoic face. There's no way out of this odd tension; no interesting topic or interruptions. To soothe the nerves, I stare at the numbers climbing up on the LED board. I stared with such anticipation, my eyes dried out. Once out of the elevator, breathing returned as a basic function. It's been a while since every nerve in my body was on high alert.

Avel stood confused beside me as I stopped in my tracks. "What are we waiting for?" he asked.

For me to get my act together.

In the end, I don't answer and fight my way to the door.

The apartment's as it was. I've been procrastinating, waiting for the right moment to start, hoping that by then I'll have the bravery to face the place. Courage doesn't erase the devastation in me when I see the glory of the wreck. But, I now know we can undo all the damages, even the strike. If Avel's strategy works, it'll be as though no incident took place.

"What should we start with?" I ask, rolling my sleeves.

I shouldn't be the one asking, but the one taking the lead, yet I find myself relying on someone other than me.

"We should make a list of the furniture

that needs replacing," he started. "Arrange for people to come pick up the selected furniture," he paced back and forth as he spoke. "Order the replacements and keep the receipts. The culprit will compensate you. Then a thorough cleaning of the place will do."

I wish I was half as composed as him. "Alright," I tell him. "I'll make the list and perhaps you could find a company that takes damaged furniture. On second thought, no company would accept goods this damaged. I reckon the garbage's our only option."

"You'd be surprised by what people are able to do with even ruins," he said, a small smile tugging at his lips.

I'm more surprised by his gentle expression and, likewise, by a hiccup from my heart.

"Let's get to work," I say in a daze.

He nods, his lips back to their usual line.

Somehow, the line looks softer. I might be lacking judgment since my mind's in a spiral.

***

I scroll on my phone, looking to buy the items on my sadly long list. I would've brought my laptop for more ease, but there's nowhere to sit. The floor itself was too soiled to sit on. I'd love to know what that black powder is. It resembles charcoal, though I ponder on the reason one would scatter charcoal everywhere. How can anyone think of this? What have I done to enrage someone to this extent?

While I'm hunting for the best deals, Avel across the room is on the phone, attempting to rid us of trash. He's leaning on the wall behind the sofa, his right leg slung forward. I'd sneak glances here and there until my eyes stopped in his direction. I began noticing things I didn't care for. The fact that his hand goes past the large phone he holds, making it seem shorter. The flow of his supple voice as he takes care of the matter.

"We have a lot of furniture. Any kind. In Every room. When is the earliest you could come? That's perfect. You'll need a big truck and a few employees. You'll be emptying the house. Trust me, you'll need as much help as you can get."

Not a minute into the staring session and I've been caught. He tilts his head, his eyebrows rising and probing. He made it easy to see the full glory of his amber eyes. I'd prefer to call them golden, since that's the colour that meets my eyes.

I shook my head and brought my attention back to the task I held. What on earth was I doing?

"Thank you. We'll see you soon," I heard him say. Then the click clacks from his shoes began to approach. "It's fixed. They'll collect the furniture today," he said, his black dress shoes in my range of vision.

"That soon?" I say, lifting my head.

"And it's completely free of charge."

"How are they earning money, then?" I say, helplessly falling into my business mindset. It's deeply ingrained in me.

"They'll refurbish what they acquired and increase its value. This deal is better for them than it is for us."

"I see. I wasn't aware of this type of business. Seems lucrative if one has the right skills. I... I," I'm losing my tracks and falling in a daze. "I'm glad the furniture will live to see another day," and I'm rambling. "Thank you for finding this solution."

"It's nothing," he said, unlike himself.

Really, who am I to judge whether it's unlike himself? What do I understand or have learned about him?

Why did the air turn stuffy making me unable to look him in the eye? My rambling's done and his curt answer, released. What else is there to say?

"You can go now," I settle with. "I'll stay to open the door to the employees. Besides, I haven't finished ordering the items on my list."

I barely bought anything because of my lack of focus.

His eyes overlapped mine, and I may be delirious, but I caught worry in them.

"I was the one to speak with them on the phone; I should stay too."

Oh.

"A-Alright then. I'll continue shopping," I say in a little voice filled with confusion.

He leaned against the wall, his head down, patiently waiting for his task. Why the same wall... We're merely centimetres away. And I wondered why the air was stuffy. Avel's not the same when he's in this apartment. He turns into a pretty decent guy. I'm not complaining, but I'm conflicted. His acts of kindness, the smiles he's been giving, the voice and the eyes I took notice of. All these little things fight for a place in my mind and I'm not ready to give in. I'd be breaking a promise with myself. As much as I try to wipe thoughts of him away, there's no stopping what my body feels. The abnormal beating of my heart. The light-headedness I have around him. The weird sensation in my stomach. I fear the effect of him.

Regardless of my feelings, he is there and I've no clue where his eyes are. I'm certainly not going to turn around to find out. If I were to, I'd need something to say. The air's awkward enough. Let's not dig deeper, and by consequence, embarrass myself.

Here I am, my finger frozen on the product page of a one seated couch I'm not planning to buy. If he looked at my screen, he'll question my hesitation over an item with no use. I suspect his silence could be proof his eyes are elsewhere. I think he'd be pretty vocal about my ability to waste time.

I'm a mess, thinking I want the banter. My mind's not rational and neither's my heart.

Chapter 21

"Hi," Laine said, her doe blue eyes in full force. The hue strikes me more than other days.

"Hi," I replied, releasing all tension.

There's no reason to be angry with her. I should be grateful she asked to meet me despite having known Auburn her entire life and me, barely a year and a half.

Shortly after the apartment was emptied, Avel and I went our separate ways and I received Laine's call. She told me she'd really like to meet. I proposed we grab a coffee at her school, knowing she's a busy college student. The establishment has a lovely coffee stand inside. This used to be our meeting place. The three of us. Auburn and I pretended to be students to blend into the flock. We'd complain that our non-existent professors gave us too many assignments while exams were looming over us. It's the closest I'd ever gotten to being a college student. I'll admit that I only experienced the fun part.

Today, I'm not able to play the part. I'm here as Rene and no one else.

"Thank you for coming," she said, her therapist tone seeping out.

"It's nothing."

"I'm aware that I shouldn't say anything on behalf of Auburn," she says, her hands gripping on the paper cup. "She should tell you herself, but I heard it didn't go well."

There's no way to know how Auburn described her botched apology. She'd shifted the blame towards me and could have well made me a villain in the story. I won't badmouth Auburn in the presence of her best friend, and I won't try to improve my image. I no longer see the need for it. My grudge, I'm afraid, is non-negotiable.

"Unfortunately, it didn't," I ultimately said, leaving nothing to linger on.

She grimaced before chugging her coffee. As though she abstained from breathing while drinking, she'd let out a long breath after.

"Shall we talk like we always did, then? Put the problems aside and speak like the friends we are?" she said.

This may be what I need as much as it is a bad idea. The problems are too relevant to be put aside. Auburn's shadow will always loom over Laine. I suppose I can make an exception for today. Today only, I'll agree on her terms and conditions, knowing I'll bail soon after. The situations's ill-fated. Laine's been nothing but a good friend to me.

"I can do that," I say, placing a hand on top of hers. For the last time, I'll feel the softness of her hand.

The corners of her lips quirked up.

"What have you been up to?" she asks,

her voice just as soft as her hand.

There's so much to tell and I'd hate to keep secrets from her, but it's for the best. These major topics would lead to commitments. She'll never leave me alone if she heard the entirety.

"Oh, you know, work and just work. I'm occupied with a new proposal I have for the office of tourism."

After the mention of the office of tourism, her eyes widen for a split second before she turned back to pretending nothing ever happened—for the sake of the conversation. This is why I'd prefer severing our ties. How long can she maintain an aloof expression? Until the pain drives her insane?

"That's great. What is it about?" she said, visibly refraining from saying all the things she'd planned to convince me with.

"I was thinking we could create tour packages and partner with local businesses so that tourists can pay a single price and visit different establishments without having to take out their wallets every time.

They'll see the true gems of the town and boost our economy at the same time."

"That's a great idea!" she exclaimed. "You must've been busy finding the gems."

"I asked nearly everyone in town for their recommendations, since I can't possibly go everywhere. There's not enough time for that."

I can't escape the awkwardness of this conversation. It's as if we were acting out the stiff script given to two officers on stake out.

"I'm sure they'll accept your proposal. They'll even wonder why it never occurred to them," she said.

"I sure hope so."

At this point, I think we both realize the small talk isn't working. Laine's expression turned grim as she released a sigh.

"Alright, Rene. Let me be honest. I'm ashamed to say that meeting you today wasn't entirely my idea. I should have called you; set a meeting with you—days ago. It doesn't matter that I'm in the middle of two fires. I should have been there for you, like I've been with Auburn this week. She asked me to check on you since she couldn't. I agreed because I felt the same. I was worried about you and us. The three of us, to be more exact. I thought I wouldn't explain things for Auburn. Alas, I have to."

Laine had reached a point where she could no longer pretend. I understand that. Honesty is a much better sight. I'll listen to her, regardless of the fact nothing she says will affect me.

I nod, signalling to her she can go ahead.

"I know Auburn like the back of my hand. The things she said that night were not her genuine thoughts. I'm sure it escalated. She said them in the heat of the moment. There's no way she'd kept all that since day one. Our laughs together were genuine. You know that; don't you?"

She looked at me, expecting a nod I couldn't give her. I sense it in my bones that what Auburn said wasn't newly created. They must have been well thought of for quite the time. They were too specific to be said *in the heat of the moment.* The hurt's already done, and the trust, broken.

Laine kept on without my nod. "She didn't mean any of it. We have to get back together and have each other's back like we always did. We aren't complete without one of us missing."

Her speech pierced my heart, poking at my multitude of scars. I'd always craved for completion within a group of people, when really, I should've sought completion within myself.

As long as I don't accept Auburn's apology, there's no way to stay by Laine's side.

I'm sorry, Laine, and even to you, Auburn, I'm sorry.

Best friends are a luxury, one I might not obtain even with the myriad of zeros in my bank account.

***

Back at my apartment building, I check the mail. There I find bills that don't scare me anymore and the classic black envelope with the authentic red seal. I guess the second meeting is looming over us. This letter is not something I can casually read on my way to my place, therefore, I hid it between my bills. I've always been careful about my surroundings, but I find myself extra paranoid nowadays. As though eyes surveyed my every move. You can't help it when you're as involved as I am. I'm in every knot of the conflict. There's always a silver lining, though. In ever bits of negativity that hit me, I've found something to rejoice over.

I hang my keys on a hook near my door and at last open the sinister envelope.

It reads:

In cause of the recent news that one of our members has fallen victim to the Crystal Mask, our second meeting has been scheduled. This, in order to share all we've gathered and to take action. The Crystal

Mask has to be stopped. As of now, we are the only ones capable of the job.

We'll meet on the next full moon at the only concert stadium our town features. Room A-184.

I hope to all see you there, once again.

The last line sent tingles down my spine. The host indeed was between us. In the worst-case scenario, they've been watching from another room, through hidden cameras. That would be straight out of a thriller. Am I in a thriller?

Aside from the tingles, the creativity of these locations never cease to surprise me. We moved from an elementary school to a concert hall. None of these are conventional. If there are no shows that night, sure it'll be empty, closed, and discreet—the perfect place, really—yet, it's ominous. All that at the hour of the dead. The flashlights still haunt the heck out of me.

With a quick research, I found that the full moon is on the 24th and that the only concert stadium in Mardi Town is called the

Blue Velvet. There's no backing out of it. What's left is to wait for that day. It occurs to me we'll have to share our findings with the group then. Yet, I recall we were all against the idea. If we collectively say we found nothing, it'll be more than suspicious —we're young, resourceful and have a police officer as a partner. We'll be identified as traitors and be burned at stakes. I can't let this happen to either of us. Surely Avel and Ace are thinking the same after receiving the letter.

I sent the two a message in our group chat to confirm. I'm still astonished Avel agreed on the group chat. He said it couldn't be helped and to blame it on efficiency.

In the matter of minutes, I'd received replies.

Ace: I am aware of the meeting. We ought to talk.

Avel: I was informed, but I'm working overtime. You can arrange the script with Ace. I'm on board with whatever you two come up with.

Here I was, thinking I could stay home for the rest of the day. No can do with all the conflicts. Life is telling me to get out of my house. Life doesn't leave me alone, not even for a second. I need my alone time to reflect and re-focus.

Ace: Let's meet at the laundromat across Eneres Street.

Looks like I can skip getting ready since I hadn't had the time to undo this morning's preparations. Also, I'm going to a laundromat, of all places. No need to touch up my hair in front of a mirror for a place where people do laundry.

Ace is either a very paranoid man or an excellent police officer. If the answer's the latter, then work must revolve around his life. Maybe that's why he has an alternate identity for his fun times. For it to not affect his work mindset. He's compelled to reinvent himself in order to do something different. While I admit he's a strange man, he's pretty interesting. The more I see him, the more odd traits I uncover. I can't say I dislike the entertainment.

Chapter 22

Despite my reluctance, I was the first to arrive at the laundromat. And there is no one here except for me. Lucky, I presume. Was this done on purpose, or is Ace good at finding places with low to no attendance? Is he lucky or strategic? I'd go with fortunate because, yes, you have the option to reserve a bar and pretend it's unpopular but a laundromat? I reckon you can't even reserve that place. For what use? A collective laundry party?

From my view of the laundromat's tall windows, I detected Ace walking the streets in quite the normal attire. Today, he's not

Ace the police officer or Ace, the club goer. He's plain Ace, with a beige coat buttoned up to the top and a brown beanie with his black hair sticking out of it.

"Sorry, I'm a bit late. Traffic," he says, stepping inside.

"You walked here," I remarked.

"The sidewalk was crowded, and every one walked at snail pace."

Let's not continue arguing with him. It'll lead nowhere. He'll always come up with an answer that won't satisfy me, but it'll shut me up.

"Let's get this meeting over with," I said, taking a seat on a bench facing the washing machines. It would have been therapeutic to look at if the machines were powered and spinning. Alas, they're as still as can be.

"I'm on it. I came prepared," he said, taking off his coat and placing it near his seat. "After some thinking, I realized we need to give them a genuine piece of information that turns out to be misleading. You understand?"

"While I understand, I can't help but wonder how we're going to find this piece of information. Can we even fool them?"

"Don't worry. Don't worry. Must I repeat myself when saying that I came prepared?" he said with a grin.

"If you had an idea already, couldn't you have sent it by text? Was this meeting necessary? Was compromising the secrecy of our meetings imperative? The members of the larger meeting aren't even supposed to have knowledge about our little matters."

"You're giving me anxiety. Those rich people will never be seen at the laundromat," he said, clutching the edge of his blouse. "Besides, I have spare time and you're not bad company. Am I bad company?"

I'll admit that half or even more than half of what I said was sarcasm. It's fun to tease Ace. His reactions are endearing and the bickering with him has another charm.

"Explain your idea, already," I said, crossing my arms, a smile escaping my lips.

"Sure, sure. I looked through the reports and remarked something all victims—except you—had in common. I was pleasantly surprised to see the latest victim also had it—"

"Wait!" I cut him off, out of extreme curiosity. "That's right! You're a police officer. You know who the latest victim is. Please tell me who it is. I won't tell a soul."

The invitation did mention the victim was part of our group, but no name had been written. I assumed I had to wait till the meeting to learn, but I'm different. I bear connections to the police—one officer. One that is investigating this affair.

"Don't even tell the person you trust the most," he then said.

"I won't."

And as if we were surrounded by people, he leaned forward and whispered in my ears. "It's Louella."

A switch flipped on in my head.

"I knew there was something fishy about her. She didn't seem capable enough to hold such a prominent position."

"If our theory is right, then yes, your intuition won," he said, nodding.

"Our theory is right," I tell him, gulping. "I forgot to mention this, but I received a letter from the Crystal Mask. He apologized to me."

"Is that so?" Ace exclaimed, jerking his head back. "That's...Surprising. Would I be able to see that letter?"

There's a strong desire within me to hold on to that letter. Would that be possible? It wouldn't be out of lack of trust. Simply out of possessiveness.

"When I get the chance, I'll show it to you," I ended up saying. An investigation is an investigation and the Crystal Mask is a criminal. No reason should be strong enough for me to omit those facts. "I have to ask you something, Ace," I say, going back to the shocking reveal. "Does Louella hold something over Avel? Because at the meeting, it looked like she had him on a leash. Avel doesn't look too good with a collar."

With that, he exploded in laughter, his

palms hitting his thighs.

"You're right, he doesn't. But no, she has nothing on Avel. He's only playing a role."

"Why does he play a role?"

"I'm not sure myself, though I know he's got a plan. There's nothing more I am able to say. But don't worry, his behaviour with Louella is nothing but a pure act. It's pretty funny too."

Real funny, I thought before realization hit.

"Now, why do you think I'm worried?" I said, feeling provoked.

He coughed. "When it comes to Avel, somehow, I think you are, and vice versa."

"It doesn't. Please, at last, elaborate on your idea so that we can go home."

"Alright, alright. For a second, I thought I was talking to Avel."

All he does is provoke me. Hit after hit, I receive, and the only way I can defend myself is by denying and changing the subject. How pathetic of me.

Seeing I was quiet after this punch, he

continued. "I noticed every house that was robbed had at least one piece of art from a certain artist with the initials S.V. With a little embellishment in our tones, we can convince them it's not a coincidence. That this artist has connections to the Crystal Mask, one way or another. Upon vaster research, I found out this artist is pretty mysterious. You can only get one of his piece at a top secret auction. If we lead them towards looking into this artist, they'll waste a lot of time only to end on a dead end."

"So you want to stall their investigation by misleading them? How are you so sure it'll lead to nothing? That artist could be linked to the Crystal Mask. Heck, he could be the Crystal Mask retrieving his stolen pieces."

"You don't own a piece of S.V. That fact alone is enough proof. We'll pretend you had a piece for the sake of royally misleading them. Besides, why would this artist feel the need to play Robin Hood? If his paintings were stolen, he could retrieve them and go on with his life. Why the robberies and good deeds?"

If I'd put in a little thought, I would've made the same conclusion. With all the information dumped on me, though, you couldn't blame me for being out of it.

Despite the proofs and the well-crafted plan, a detail of it bothers me.

"What if they ask me about the painting?"

"That's something I'm still thinking of because those paintings are extremely exclusive. You can't even find pictures online to replicate them," he says, scratching the back of his head.

His answer struck me like lightning, igniting a sudden idea.

It is now my turn to show intelligence.

"If that's the case, nobody could have knowledge of my so-called piece. They'd have never seen it and won't be able to doubt my description. I won't need to show it either, since the Crystal Mask supposedly stole it. Unless the Crystal Mask himself publicly denies I had that painting, none can say a thing.”

“That’s fixed, then. Still, you ought to be careful. You don’t know what these rich people are capable of if they see through the lie,” he said, his eyes suddenly turning into stone.

My toes curled at the sight. I wouldn’t know unless I fell into their trap. One wrong step and it seems I’m bound to meet the grim reaper. Money is dangerous. Money is capable of creating a living hell. If Ace’s usually cheery eyes turn this serious, then it must be true.

Does it matter that I’m officially petrified? I’ve gone too far to ponder about that.

Chapter 23

Work is still my priority. The Crystal Mask and his investigation won't stop me from doing what I do best. Hence, after the meeting at the laundromat—weird thing to say—I headed home and printed out my completed proposal. Most of my past nights were spent compiling all the ideas I'd gathered to create a decent proposal I'd then give to the director of the tourism office.

I can't wait to collect the fruits of my hard work. There's no way this the project flunks. In no alternate universe, could this go wrong. It'll make my day and allow me to forget all that went wrong in the span of a month. My days will turn golden as they were.

I walked to the office of tourism and was greeted by the secretary with the phony smile.

"It has been a while, Ms. Mint."

"It has." I gave her a nod. "I'm here to meet with Mr. Maddox."

Naturally, I'd given a glance at Auburn's office when I came in, out of habit.

One day, I might become so aloof that I'll look at the office out of boredom and it won't affect me at all. It won't be a pin striking my body or even the light touch of a finger. Completely weightless.

"You're in luck, Ms. Mint. He happens to be free at the moment. If you'd please follow me," she said, taking off.

Soon.

Soon.

Soon enough, I'll be flourishing anew.

"Here we are," she said, before eclipsing herself, leaving a whiff of her floral perfume in the air.

"Rene?" he said, sitting behind his desk. "My! It's been a while. Come in. Come in."

After some time collaborating with the tourism office, I've been trusted enough to directly go through the director—Mr. Maddox—whenever I have a proposal. They have faith in my ideas. That is how I eventually became acquainted with him. My name is a free pass to the director's office. That alone brings back the confidence I witnessed flying away in the past days. It's all coming back to me now.

I dropped my document on his desk, cutting straight to the chase. I know that the second he reads the introduction alone, he'll be hooked. He'll be going on and on with praises.

I watch as he flips open the file. His pupil moves left and right and, as expected, he flips it closed after the first page. He handed me the file and left me puzzled. Wouldn't he need to keep it for records?

"There must have been a miscommunication," he said. "Auburn already gave this idea. She must've asked you to hand it for her, in case she was too busy. And I assume she was too busy to tell you she had the time to present it herself. The idea's great, though! I was so happy with Auburn's work that I promoted her." Mr. Maddox said, his eyes wide and glowing.

Miscommunication? It's not even a misunderstanding. I crafted the idea on my own and that after our fight. She couldn't have known—

"Oh, I see. If she already gave hers, then you wouldn't need mine after all. I'm sorry for taking up your time," I say, forcing a smile.

"No, no, it's alright. You're welcome anytime."

I left the office and I'm sure I'll find it challenging to ever step foot there again.

Turns out Auburn sent Laine to spy on me. Not to know if I was doing well. It's obvious she's given up on us. So much so that she's decided to send one last hit my way. She chose to get something out of it before it ended for good. Are those her true colours?

I let her have it as a parting gift. I'm giving her a sweet promotion and accepted the bitter strike she'd call a gift.

I can let go now. I can call this the ending of our story. Life differs from novels and happy endings are never guaranteed.

If I told the truth to Mr. Maddox, it would be my word against hers and the fight would persist. We'll argue for additional reasons and become enemies. Let's not wage war over something petty. What she stole wasn't petty, but the act was.

All I can do is grieve what could have been. My triumph... I might not benefit from the event at all. Auburn proved herself to be capable of sabotaging me. Wouldn't she go as far as recommending hotels in the brochure instead of my properties? That would render the time I spent planning a waste. Auburn foreshadowed my ups and downs and took on the mission to be the instigator of the downs.

***

I had to dig deeper into my stress relief methods. On nights where I truly feel like trash, alcohol seems weak and cigarettes, an appetizer. So I press on the lowest button of the elevator, it drops me off to the garage.

While I prefer to walk in Mardi Town—since taking taxis or maintaining a car seems like a waste of money here—I do own a sort of vehicle. The snowy and icy weather doesn't offer the best conditions for it, hence I keep it away for the season. During the year, I use it sparsely on the days I need to pop the cap off. I then release all of my bottled emotions. I'll brave the cold and the slippery roads, making an exception to my rule, given that I've reached my limit.

I walk alone in the chilly and dim garage to get to my spot, number 5034.

There waits for me, my baby. My black cruiser. On that bike, I have the impression that the word freedom was invented for my sake.

Lifting the seat, I take out my helmet and wear it right away. Not only does it serve as protection, but it gives me reassurance. No one will know the identity of the woman on the motorcycle. I can shout like a lunatic and the people judging won't have a name or face to put their judgments onto. It's akin to being invisible.

The moment I settle onto the bike, I can hear my breath shake. It's not the nerves, but the emotions that are preparing to spill. The thrill of a ride should bring euphoria, but on days of high stress, I know I'll be tasting heaven and hell, back and forth.

As I insert the key, the revving sound of the motor penetrates deep into my soul. The vibrations shake me to the core. I twist the handle and make my way out to see the city lights.

Thanks to my helmet, the wind feels bearable. Although it can sneak onto my face through openings near my neck, I'm fine. Without the helmet, the wind, ice cold, would mess with my eyes and I wouldn't see the road.

I'm well into it, my back arched upwards and chest leaning forward. At three in the morning, the only ones out are ones with bad intentions—you'd think. Though true, you can also find a few like me who dream of freedom or escape. What better way to taste liberty than riding a motorcycle when everyone's asleep?

There's a place I find comfort in. One not accessible to pedestrians. All my bike rides end there.

The road is pretty spine-tingling on its own, but I know arriving there is the true climax. It's an anticlimactic climax because of its calm nature, yet still the highest point of the night. I'm going below the bridge, where a minimal amount of cars pass by. Somehow I'm safe there.

The road was quiet until I heard a familiar motor sound. The sound was identical to mine, but it was coming from behind. I looked over discreetly and, as if I'd been cloned, next to me was the same motorcycle as me. Same model, same colour. The driver wore all black clothing and so did I. I'd wanted to blend in with the night. That person nearly succeeded too. Were it not for the sound of their bike, I'd think they were the night.

What a coincidence. That person leaves me curious, while the road is where I should have my eyes on.

As though we were headed to the same place, the motorcycle remained on my trail. There's nowhere to turn if I feel threatened; the road's straight. On the flip side, I'm on a black bike, wearing black clothing, and I mean no harm. This opens possibilities for my clone to be just as harmless. Or not. Positive possibilities co-exist with negative ones.

I'll stop under the bridge soon enough. If they stop too, I'll know to dash away.

Slowly but surely, they were on the other side of the road, far from me. We were travelling at roughly the same speed, occasionally glimpsing at each other out of the corner of our eyes. When came the time to stop right under the bridge, I was surprised to see they did as well. But we're so far from each other, I have nothing to fear. Like true clones, it's possible we initially had the same idea. That person could have switched lanes to give me space or have their space to let off steam.

Once I've climbed off my cruiser, I remove my helmet and let it hang on a handle. Then comes the time where I lean my back on the bridge wall and bask in the dead of the night. For the first time, the winter air I despised feels refreshing. I could almost mistake the moment for an extra chilly summer night.

On the other end, that person removed their helmets as well. It makes no difference, since the bridge doesn't have lights underneath it. Robert could be the motorcycle guy and I wouldn't recognize him.

Just then, a car with their headlights lit at full power passed by their lane and allowed me to get a peek. The car zipped by so fast, I could barely make out a feature. A pair of plump lips.

Intrigued, I leaned forward and waited for another car to pass. When the next one came, I saw eyes. Those I recognized. How could I not when those eyes were golden and empty? I grew concerned because I've never seen them filled with so much void. Without thinking, I took out my phone and sent a message to the man standing meters away.

Me: Are you all right?

In the absence of light, I can't see if he's looking my way. I scc an all black silhouette and that's all.

Avel: I have a lot on my mind.

He answered without questions. I'm certain he spotted me as well, illuminated by the glow of a passing car.

For a while, I won't pry either. It's clear we're both here for some peace and quiet. I set aside my phone and continued to stare into the darkness. This place is my reset button. It's where I forgive and forget. All for my own good. The next morning, I'll be back. I'll focus more on work than emotions, seeing that they ruin everything. I'll maintain the only relationships I can trust are here to stay and find myself somewhere.

Sometimes I find the silence to be unbearable and on other occasions I find it is what I longed for all my life. Tonight, it's the latter. I'm not scared of the lack of sound. Despite the late hour, I don't think of the night as sinister. I think of it as an embrace. When the night lets go, it'll take a layer of my soul with it. These words sound poetic, but really, it's my commitment.

When I see Avel in the distance, I imagine he must have come here as often as I did. Never having crossed paths is just as strange as suddenly meeting everywhere. In Java Haze too, we're regulars that never noticed the other. It's funny to know we were at the same places but never laid eyes on one another because of our lack of interest in people.

We can still enjoy silence by conversing through text messages, no? I come here to reflect, perhaps shout a little, cry a river, let out some steam. Having Avel here with me prevents me from doing those things. Might as well let it out another way.

Me: Are you here to relieve stress?

Avel: I suppose.

It's hard to reply when his words are so short.

I have the odd impulse to complain to him. To talk about everything that is bothering me and swear to never mention it again. Could I find it in me to confide in Avel? He's no friend, nor is he a fiend—not anymore. He's nothing, yet something.

If he'd send me a message asking about what's wrong, I wouldn't hesitate long. He's Avel. He won't ask about my feelings. Why would he? Let's not even dream about it.

"Could I talk with you?" I say out loud while writing the message.

I nearly dropped my phone when he'd sent a response.

Come over, he wrote.

Chapter 24

And so I did. Two words from his part and I settled on my motorcycle. It's possible that I broke a few traffic laws while crossing the street because getting there legally would have taken too long. I only sped up to not risk getting hit by a car —it's an empty road, but you never know.

I parked my bike next to Avel's. I don't want to take off my helmet. It's perfectly hiding my eyes and expression. He would be clueless as to where to stare and I won't be confronted with a glare that'd bare me. Just like the night leaves me vulnerable, so does he. I had a quick peek before turning off the motor. Once I turn it off, the bike won't emit light and we'll barely see a thing. I guess I won't need the helmet after all.

Avel remained unfazed by the rumble of my bike or the glare of its headlights. I seized the moment to get a good glimpse. He wore something much different from usual. A turtle neck and a leather jacket. His clothes cling to him, exposing a figure I had never witnessed because of his oversized suits. Before I could go further, he turned, his golden eyes stern.

"Aren't you going to turn off your motor?" he said.

"I am," I replied in a haste.

My embarrassment outweighs my anger.

I took off my helmet and leaned on his wall—leaving a little distance between us.

My eyes on the road, I take out of my pocket a pack of what looks like cigarettes, but in reality, they're lollipops. I've been tempted lately and find that they're the only ones that calm me down. I hid them in an empty pack of cigarette to give a false sense of satisfaction to my brain.

"Would you like one?" I ask him, oblivious to what else I could say.

"What an interesting method to quit smoking. I should take lessons," he said, grabbing a watermelon lollipop.

I took the cherry.

"You smoke?" I ask.

"It was a mistake to start," he says, unwrapping the candy and popping it in his mouth.

I can't help but agree. Cigarettes never ceased the stressed. The act was placebo until it became a vicious cycle. Smoking caused me more stress than work itself after a while.

The taste of artificial cherry is much more pleasant than tobacco. It doesn't soil my lungs and gives me sweet nostalgia. My memories aren't the best, but even I had sweet moments.

"You must be stressed if you're under a bridge at three in the morning," I tell him.

"A lot is happening."

"You can tell me about it and we'll have

a fair exchange.”

He scoffed. “We don’t always have to do business.”

“We never really got to do business since you refused my loan.”

He fell silent.

“I’ll start,” I say. “Despite the various events that occurred, which you are familiar with, they were not enough to bring me here. I settled with those problems. I accepted them. Then came the cherry on top and it got out of hand.”

“If you keep using so many metaphors, I won’t understand a thing.”

“But you did.”

He took a lick of his candy. “Keep on.”

“I’ve lost two people dear to me. They’re not dead. They’re well; too well even. I’m thinking I lost them more than they’ve lost me. They left me stumped. Did they not genuinely love me like I did? After all had been said and I was ready to let go, they hit me with one last punch in the gut. They switched entirely and betrayed me.” I’m emotionless when I say this. Purely because

I am exhausted.

"They've done you a favour to reveal themselves," he said. "Had it lasted ages, you'd be in ruins by the end of it."

The undeniable truth leaves a lingering sting to my scars.

"The year for me was good. Only then could I say my entire year was relatively happy. It's weird to say, but I wished the lie would go on for longer, so that I could stay a happy fool. My healthy support system is gone. Gone when I need it the most. You can't blame me for being attached to fiction."

"I don't blame you," he said, his voice calm. "Believing in a lie won't do you any good, but I can understand. Our world is a horrible place to live in and I'm reminded of it every day."

That's a pretty dark thing to say. I've thought the same thing for years until I moved here and started to experience life in its full glory. Even as I resort to unhealthy coping methods, I still see the world in multi-colour, while Avel appears to observe it in black and white. It's a question of perspectives.

"Why do you stay in a world you think is horrible, then?" that is a dark question for me to ask, but I can't beat curiosity. I want to understand why he lives and fulfills his duties towards a society he despises with passion.

"There are some matters I have to take care of."

I won't pry seeing he didn't elaborate.

"Are these matters not going well?" I can at least get him to share the burden of his emotions.

Tonight, in a tightly fitted leather jacket, he's presented bare and vulnerable. In the darkness, I can vaguely make out lines of his body. I almost want to trace those lines.

"They're going as they were always going. It's just tiring." Those words he said while exhaling ever so slowly.

I don't know what he's going through, yet I feel the exhaustion. He's making me remember things of the past. He's making my heart turn into mush.

"I get it," I said, without thinking.

"You get it?" he asked, turning to me.

Even in the darkness, I can grasp the gold in his eyes. I can only see his eyes now.

"I get it," I repeated, in a trance.

"Who were you Rene Mint?"

"Someone I'd like to forget."

"Why?" he then asked, his eyes deep in mine.

"I wasn't proud of her and nobody was either," I answered, almost hypnotized.

"That person's still there. You're an improved version, which did good to come here and did no wrong in choosing friends."

That's out of character for you, Avel.

Regardless, it doesn't change my mind. I was wrong. My judgment was lacking. I shouldn't have trusted people so easily and believed they cared. I should have questioned the authenticity of their words and actions. I was too hasty and accepted the first people that approached me.

"I was in the wrong," I say, desperately blaming myself.

"You were not," he nearly shouted. "Some things are beyond our control."

"Do I let everything go and consider it of the past?" I ask, my voice quivering—not from the cold, but from the nerves.

"Occasionally you do. Some fights are not worth the efforts. It doesn't make you weak to walk away from these fights. On the contrary, that shows you're intelligent."

"When do you know if the fight's worth it or not?"

He put his hand on my shoulder, "Look in their eyes," he said, staring into mine, "and you'll either see a flame of hatred strong enough to give you the strength to fight or a flame so blue you'd want to move on."

In his eyes, I see no flame of hatred or passive blue flame. But there is a flame, flickering like no other. I wish for insanity and nothing else. The thought of his hand stroking my hair runs free in my mind and I realize how warm he'd made me feel. His hand remained on my shoulder and I settled for that touch. I'd be crazy to ask more of him when unsure of my own intentions.

My heart completely melted when he'd started smiling. He softly curved his lips, and a hidden dimple made an appearance. Who can say they saw Avel being so sweet? Perhaps just me. That smile is hard to handle. It's so far from his usual persona that this might just be the true one.

In disbelief, I laugh lightly.

He drops his hand back to his side and turns to the road, a content look on his face.

"What is it you don't know, Avel Malt?"

"Many things. I'm human too, you know."

"It's only tonight I'm realizing you are."

"What was I before?"

Hesitancy crept in but the night makes me vulnerable enough to spill the beans.

"A demon."

He faced me, his lips pursed and his eyebrows raised, "A demon?" he exploded in laughter, his cackles making their way one by one to my ears.

"I had the feeling you didn't like me, but a demon never crossed my mind," he said between laughs.

I've always wondered, when falling for someone, do you hear a bell ring or make a pro and con list? Does the heart flutters at the action of that person or the person itself? I can't say that the questions vanished, for I'm still just as confused. Yet I know for sure Avel did something to me. It shouldn't be the case, but it is. I've been falling for a while, in all the wrong places. Now in front of Avel, it's as if I'm falling in a hole tenderly carved for my sake.

Chapter 25

Days were spent at ease without cherry lollipops or glasses of whisky. They were mundane. After an eventful couple of days, you start to crave the days where the worst thing to happen is for your coffee to turn cold. I couldn't agree more with the saying 'no news is good news'.

My mind's been preoccupied, yes, but only with someone. The idea of him invaded my head. It pushed away all other thoughts and became the sole notion. I'm having daydreams about what could be when I know it won't be.

The movie that played in my head

wasn't too bad. I'd rate it at least 4.5 stars. It even changed me for the better. I found myself smiling at strangers on the streets. My cheery mood is to blame, for sure. All because of Avel's hidden facade. Who knew he could be so soft, so wise, so...nice.

We're moving on because movies are fiction. I've been productive; ordered all the furniture and made sure they were placed correctly in the apartment. Now I'm back in business. No news from the police yet about the culprit. I don't know what I'll do when they find them. How far will I go to ruin this person? I'll need to get my money back because I suffered a loss from this ordeal. I had to replace almost everything. The cries of my bank account echo in my dreams. I awoke in cold sweats after a dream where a few zeros were missing from my balance. My half-awake-self had to check my account. At first, I was relieved the zeros weren't missing, but the list of numerous transactions broke me. Minus this. Minus that...

After leaving my home, I go downstairs

to see if there is any mail. Shocker, there's another black envelope. Doesn't faze me anymore. The letters and the meetings are becoming a joke. I'm not sure why I'm still attending. I could bail, but I won't. They're a free source of entertainment. I don't want to miss the moment they gobble up our misleading tip. There's something else I wouldn't want to miss. He's not a something. He's Avel. I'll get to sit next to him in this meeting, along with Ace. I'm ashamed to admit I want to talk with him, laugh with him and exchange eye contact. Of course, we'll laugh after the meeting to not blow our covers. The meeting between partners thrills me more than the main meeting itself.

The letter was simply a reminder of our meeting tonight. Whoever sent the mail must think we're stupid to the extent we'll fail to remember this *prominent* day. The more letters sent, the higher risks we have of attracting suspicion. That being said, I stuffed the envelope in my bag when a woman came downstairs for her mail. I don't know whether I should keep these letters somewhere safe or burn them. Their origin is still unknown while their presence is incriminating.

***

With time to spare before midnight, I found myself a table at Java Haze to get some work done. There, I picked up today's journal and was surprised to spot an article talking about the Crystal Mask's latest activities. My eyes grew wider when reading the victim's name. Ace had already told me it was Louella, but that was private information. Who are these journalists and who's the rat? Karma's what I'd call this. From the get-go, I didn't like how close she stuck to Avel and how she squirmed in her seat. I grinned like a fool, holding up the paper. Robert tilted his head at me and I ignored him, burrowing my face deeper in the article. This piece of news can possibly cause her more damage than the burglary itself, and I'm all for it.

***

As night time crept up, I nervously approached the concert hall, feeling a slight chill in the air. It's been days since I met with Avel and even more since I saw any member of our secret meetings. I don't want to be intimidated like last time. They might be richer and more powerful than me I but we're all human. Their worth doesn't give them superpowers. I might even be better since my business's ethical. In contrast, Louella's flaws lie in her business and personality. So, inside out.

"Rene?" I hear a voice call from behind.

I turn and meet our unofficial leader, Mr. Moss—the ex chief of police. Since when were we on a first name basis? Is it because I could be the same age as his daughter?

"Hello, Jorge," I say, a smile so very

amused drawing on my face.

I refuse to let him have his way. Those meetings didn't turn us into acquaintances. After we're done, I'm not planning to see the man again.

He obviously looked startled hearing someone so young talk this casually.

He lingered for a moment before speaking again, pretending all was well. "Did the investigation go well with your partners?"

"It wasn't easy, but I think we've found something useful."

"I can't wait to hear it," he says, his face solemn without a hint of excitement.

From his perspective, besides catching the Crystal Mask, nothing about this grim situation would be joyful.

"Let's go inside," he says.

Once inside, we've made our way to a door called A-184 as mentioned in the letter. All day I'd wonder how we'd be seated. In a concert stadium, I can only presume we'll have an empty hall with red seats all facing the stage. Would we all sit in the same row or would we be divided in the hall? We wouldn't face each other and that might be for the best considering that a majority of the people there I'd rather not face.

To my surprise, behind the door, A-184 wasn't a hall with rows of red seats and a stage but a mundane meeting room you'd find in most offices. This time, the lights were on and no one was holding a flashlight under their heads.

Madame Sophie waved at me from her seat, Mr. Blankship sitting next to her. Not too far from them were Mr. Shaefer and the sneering Louella. The sight of me just annoyed her that much. I'm flattered.

I sat on the opposite side and left exactly two seats on my sides, knowing Avel and Ace will be with me instead of the people that dragged them to the meetings. Now, Louella can be the one to watch with envy. She'll be squirming in her seat for different reasons.

Mr. Moss sat down near Louella, waiting for his partner, Ms. Riel. After came Mr.

Moore and the mysterious Mr. Pacheco. They settled in the centre of the table. Nobody was late. We were mostly early. A little shy from twelve.

"Rene!" I heard Ace shout.

Behind me were the familiar faces I'd waited for. Ace looked ecstatic to see me, and Avel acknowledged me with a nod. An improvement. He tends to hide part of himself when in larger groups and unveil it in the company of few trusted people. I find this more flattering than Louella's annoyance towards me. He's at ease with me. Yet I'm not. I've intruded his world through my imagination for who knows how long these days. My perception of him was altered and I'm not sure I can handle sitting so close to him.

The moment he sat down, my theory was proven to be faulty. His body close to mine brought warmth and comfort. I let my shoulders drop and instantly felt in security. With Avel by my side, there's no need to fear those people who like to pick on me.

Who'd guessed I'd do a one eighty with my opinion? I remember the day where I wished to be Mr. Pacheco's partner instead —I still do. His aura never ceases to intrigue me. If I investigated with him, I'd know of his businesses and work secrets by now. While it's regrettable, I have no complaints about my current partners.

The meeting begun with Jorge Moss's guidance. His chin lifted and his breaths harsh, he said, "another member has fallen victim to the despicable Crystal Mask. We ought to take action! I now ask of you to share all you've gathered since our first meeting. It is imperative to include every single detail and not leave anything out."

I hadn't experienced any guilt when he had been so vocal about being completely honest. Other than my partners, none felt trustworthy.

Mr. Moore was the first to speak. He beat around the bush for minutes, before ultimately admitting to have found nothing. He said the information was limited and there was nothing we weren't already aware of. His partner, Mr. Pacheco, remained silent, his expression hidden under his sunglasses.

Madame Sophie and Mr. Blankship were next. They cast a quick glance downwards prior to admitting defeat.

"It's futile," Madame Sophie said. "What did you expect us to do? We have connections, enough to fund an investigation, but in the end there's nothing. I might even say that it's beyond our control."

Mr. Blankship continued, "To say that it's beyond our control is insulting yet true. We're much better with inside jobs. People like us taking revenge or wanting to take down an empire that is threatening theirs. The Crystal Mask is an outsider. We can't track him down."

Seeing the worried looks every one exchanged, I realize I might be the only thinking that statement was pretty funny.

"I'm looking forward to our trio of youngsters; they even have a police officer in the team. They'll be the ones to give us hope," the unofficial host said with the first smile of the night.

And the show begins, I thought, peeking at both Avel and Ace.

Chapter 26

"We do have a lead," I say and watch as their bodies press forward. "With Ace's help, we established what every victim had in common. A particular item the Crystal Mask never failed to steal."

I handed the baton to Ace since he made the discovery.

"Every victim owned a painting from the artist S.V. All were stolen, without exception."

The room kept quiet. Avel took that as a cue. He missed the meeting where we concocted our deception, but he was briefed on the details.

"The artist's connection to the Crystal Mask is a possibility. Taking a broader perspective, they might even turn out to be the Crystal Mask."

"That's going really far," Mr. Moore said, laughing.

Avel didn't accept his laughter and kept on, "The theory suggests the artist is conscious of few individuals that illicitly distribute copies of their work to unsuspected buyers by taking advantage of the fact the paintings are displayed nowhere."

If someone had questioned me about the lead, I would have frozen. Avel's either well prepared or naturally intelligent. I'd believe either option.

"How would you know their paintings are that exclusive? You're a plus one. You're not rich and will never have the chance to attend an auction, let alone afford a painting," Ms. Riel said, a hard edge to her voice.

They defend this artist as if their symbol of wealth is at stake. How else will they show off their fortune if not with a virtually unobtainable painting?

He directed his gaze to me as he said, "I learned all about it from Ms. Mint, who owned an S.V. Painting."

Before they could contest, Ace came to the rescue: "I mentioned earlier that all victims had a painting."

All those who had their mouths open, closed them. There's nothing they can say when a police officer confirmed it. Now I'm guilty. Ace has just betrayed his promise of office by telling this lic. From the beginning, that was his idea. And I agree with thinking white lies are needed to combat greater lies made by corrupted people.

"How do you intend we find the artist when they're such a private person?" Mr. Blankship said.

"If there is one person in this room that hasn't been to the auction yet, now would be the time," I said, looking around at their nervous faces.

"Who hasn't attended?" I ask and hands

were reluctant to raise. The act of admitting is humiliating to them. They all want to pretend they're up to these ridiculous standards. And so I had to add, "That person could be our key to finding the Crystal Mask." I felt like a mother motivating her children.

"I haven't been yet," Mr. Moore says, his hand reaching the sky.

They are just as childish as I had expected.

"Perfect. We'll join forces to get you an invitation. Then we'll make progress." Jorge Moss said, clasping his hands. After a few insignificant remarks from the nobles, we decided to wrap up the meeting and call it a day. The gathering was brief because of their lack of progress. They'll be disappointed to know our progress will also turn out to be a waste of time.

"They gobbled it right up. We didn't need to worry," Ace told me as we walked the empty streets.

"I was impressed by Avel's little ad lib," I say, looking at my left where Avel is.

With a bashful expression, he managed to muster a shy smile.

Amidst the laughter and smiles, as we recalled our lie and their response to it, a sudden reminder jolted me back to reality.

"What do we do now?" I say. "We gave them something to bite on to leave the Crystal Mask alone because he's commendable, yes. But there's something off about this. Don't we have to uncover who he is?"

The sombre road that was previously filled with the sound of our laughter grew quiet. Maybe they realized the purpose of our meetings had always been to uncover the Crystal Mask's identity. The idea indeed tugs on a heart string. The Crystal Mask, from my eyes, is an activist silently screaming for a cause. To take that away from him doesn't feel right either.

We can't forget his methods are improper. I'm not one to be good, but this is conflicting. Avel and Ace appeared to be just as conflicted as I am. They're walking silently, hands held behind their backs.

Telephone ring the unknown. My friends won't leave me alone…

My ringtone played while I sat by the kitchen counter, indulging in a toast and eggs. I dropped the toast and sluggishly went to pick up my phone I'd left near the window. The name written on the screen makes me want to throw the phone away. I chose to do the complete opposite and answered the call.

"Hello," I say, trying my best to not sound angry. She doesn't deserve to hear my wrath or my sadness. Few people do anymore. If they don't want to see me happy, then they have no right to see me dejected.

"Rene! Thank you for picking up," Laine said. "I just had to call you because I learned of what Auburn did. It's horrible, and I didn't know she'd use what I told her against you. It's completely unacceptable," she said, her voice rushed.

Like I'd believe that. They're eternal best friends. They're unable to hide secrets from each other. Laine is being sent by Auburn once again to stay in contact with me and collect all the essential information.

I kept quiet to see if she had something else to say before I end the call.

"You do know me, Rene? I would never do something like this. I genuinely was concerned for you and curious about your work that day. Even Auburn, she was overwhelmed and acted on impulse. We can fix this."

I started to believe she was honest. That she didn't come with hidden intentions. But when she defended Auburn, I knew the truth mattered little at this point. Laine is blinded by her longtime friendship and there's no fixing that. She will eventually come to understand it one day.

It's definitely not my responsibility. Regardless, I need to distance myself from these two.

"There's nothing to fix, Lane. I hope they teach you at school that therapists are not magic worker and some things can't be fixed. It's always up to us. Give up for my own good and yours. Don't feel bad, just let go."

After ending the call, I made sure to block both of them. That way, I won't receive calls or messages that are bound to make me hesitate. That officially concludes it.

I can't even have eggs on toast in peace nowadays. I ate the remains which turned cold. And I can't stay home all day, lazing around. Though I could. The places I rent make money by themselves at times. I don't have to check them every day, but I do. Because I like to be productive and can't binge watch a show for the life of me with my short attention span. Compared to older days, this lifestyle for me is paradise. I live in my Utopia.

***

I walk through downtown streets, my coat wavering from the wind, a coffee cup in my hand and work that keeps me abundant on my mind. What more could I want? I'm grateful for this life, even if I lost friendships along the way. I am content with having had the chance to experience something I didn't dare ask. All I dare ask is not to be pulled back to the past. That place for me was torture. Any trigger brings me the taste of hell.

It was futile to ask. Bitterness filled my mouth, and I stopped in my tracks, having lost control of my limbs. There's nowhere to go. I can't go anywhere. I can't move. Fear is holding me down. I'm faced with the very person who sent me the letter that brought me to tears not long ago. He had on an innocent smile. The kind you give to a friend you haven't seen in ages and are genuinely delighted to see. It might be the case for him. As for me, I want to be kidnapped by aliens. Right now!

"Audra! I'm so happy to see you again," he said.

His voice gave me shivers that ran deep.

"You had me worried there when you didn't respond to my letter."

'You psycho!' I want to shout. But I can't. My voice isn't coming out.

He moved forward, closing the gap between us with each step. Instinctively, I should've stepped back. I'm powerless.

"Are you so happy to see me you're crying?" he said, amused.

Tears just fell on their own. He reaches a hand to my cheek and I flinch. His hand is merely a millimetre away from my skin before it is slapped away by another.

I'm pulled back and stare at the source, Avel. He stood, tightness in his eyes and lips that flattened.

"Who are you?" Claud said, looking intensely at Avel.

"You don't need to know," he answered.

"What do you m—" before Claud could finish, Avel grabbed my wrist and pulled me along.

"Don't look back," he said, his grip soft and warm.

Avel is no alien, but he's doing the trick. He's an option I hadn't dared to wish for since I thought it impossible. Seems that when I'm with him, the impossible becomes possible.

Chapter 27

I'd sampled poison for a minute there. It lingers and propagates all over. One taste was enough to remember it all. To give me whiplash. To bring me back to the hard times and mostly to the old me. Rene Mint would have never frozen on the spot. But Audra Frye would have. I'd lost Rene Mint for a minute or two after having encountered someone who knew and harmed Audra Frye.

Now I'm in limbo. I'm neither Audra nor Rene. I find it hard to come back.

Maybe he'll tell the others and they'll find me. Then I'll be standing face to face with the ones I vowed to never see again. My personal hell had been their creation. My childhood and teenage years were wasted because of them. In Mardi Town, I picked up the pieces and somehow made myself whole. Now an earthquake of emotion is threatening to crumble them back.

Maybe that's my comfort zone. I'm afraid of being pulled back to that world and accept it because it's familiar. What pulls me now is Avel. With complete reliance on him, I allowed him to pull me along.

Soon enough, he paused at Lost Street.

"What are we doing here?" I ask, my voice rather broken from all the tears.

"I live here," he said.

This brought all the water back into my eyes. He took me to his building.

"Why..." I asked, wary.

"Follow me."

I have no other choice when his hand was still gripping my wrist.

"It's the only place that gives us

privacy," he added.

Why do we need privacy in the first place? I don't dare to ask. Something about his tone keeps me silent. On second thought, I won't deny that privacy sounds nice right now. I'm a wreck from all the tears and the fear that petrified me. A trip to the bathroom to refresh would be nice, yes.

We entered his apartment, and it's nothing like I imagined—not that I ever pictured the place. His place is as simple as vanilla ice cream. The walls are white and without a single picture frame. The sofa's beige without a coloured pillow. The kitchen looks like it's never been used, it's without a plate in the sink. Despite spending most of his time at home, the place doesn't appear to be lived in.

"Make yourself at home," he said, bewildering me further.

"Where's the bathroom?" I ask.

"The first door on the left," he pointed for me.

I try to take a step, but a weight I forgot

about anchored me down. The grip felt natural, as if it had always been there. Avel hasn't noticed. He looks at me, his eyes soft. I direct my eyes downward to signal the problem. His attention there, he pulls his arm in a swift movement.

"Sorry," he says.

There's nothing to be sorry about, I'd like to tell him. He saved me. His hold brought me comfort. Instead of words, I conveyed my feelings to him with a smile.

With my wrist cold from the absence of his touch, I stare at my reflection in the bathroom mirror. The strength in my eyes seemed to have faded, causing them to droop and appear heavy. The fright I had just experienced left me with a pale complexion. Water can't fix those problems. Only time can. In the end, all I did in the bathroom was tie my hair. Having nothing else to do, I went back to the living room where Avel awkwardly sat.

Why did he bring me here instead of a coffee shop? I could've composed myself there too. I would've been comfortable even. Here, I'm nervous and I overthink.

Do I sit next to him?

Do I stand?

The sofa only has two seats...

It'd be odd to not sit either.

And so I did.

"Aren't you going to ask?" I say, holding my breath from the close contact.

"Sharing is optional, but you're welcome to do it."

"I could share, yes."

"You don't have to," he said, turning to face me. While doing so, he brushed my elbow by accident. That sent a jolt of electricity through my arm.

"Sorry," he whispered.

I waved my hand, showing him I'm fine.

Sitting side by side on the sofa, I can't help but notice the tension between us, a tension that somehow provides coziness. It's been a while since I last experienced this.

"The guy you saw there. We dated in the past. I consider it the biggest mistake of my life."

He acknowledged silently with a nod.

"The second biggest mistake was not leaving my hometown earlier. I could've been richer and happier longer."

"What made you change your name, Audra Frye?" he said.

When he'd said my full name, every hair on my body rose. That name threatened to bring out a very weak person. It's likely that Avel was listening since the beginning. But it's impossible for him to have heard my last name since Claud never mentioned it.

I looked at him, an eyebrow raised. He doesn't seem to realize what he'd said. I'll brush it off for now, but not for long. I have questions too.

"My mother made me change my name. After something she'd said, I knew I couldn't take it anymore."

"What did she say?"

"You were a mistake, Audra Frye. That last blow made me buy a train ticket. And when I arrived in Mardi Town, I figured it'd be best to change everything so that I never have to remember."

"Must've been tough."

Indeed.

It never was easy to feel like a burden to everyone. To feel you didn't belong. That no one truly cared for you. That you weren't worth any of these people. I grew out of it, though, and realized they're the ones that didn't deserve me. They treated me like garbage on a daily basis and never were apologetic for it.

"What did he do then, the guy that called you Audra?"

Avel caught me off guard. He's not one to show interest or to be remotely curious. I haven't known him for long, but I might be witnessing Avel opening up. It's exciting. Makes me want to tell him everything about me. So I oblige.

"His name is Claud, not that it matters. He was the only person I thought genuinely cared for me, yet he looked down on me, as did the rest. When I realized I wasn't properly cared for, it was too late. He wouldn't let me leave. I'll leave the rest to your imagination."

"You shouldn't, Rene, you shouldn't. Letting my imagination run free makes me want to kill the guy," he said, his hand gripping tight the sofa.

"He's already dead to me. You don't have to do a thing," I say in an attempt to appease him.

I'm surprised by his flared up eyes and the veins sticking out his arm. That's a genuine reaction. You couldn't physically feign concern. I have an eye for discerning truth and false. Avel was a little difficult because his eyes hid emotions perfectly. Now, I'm amazed at how much they express.

"Do you know why he's in town?" he said, visibly trying to keep calm.

"He sent me a letter days ago. I don't know how he got my address or my current name. He wrote that he overlooked my worth before, but always knew I'd make a fortune someday. I threw the letter without sending him a reply and failed to consider he'd come all the way here."

I was so stupid. Of course, he'd do something if he heard nothing back. He has my address, that alone is dangerous. He could be waiting at my door at this very moment. What if he's been there all morning and followed me till we could *coincidentally* meet? I'm the one holding on tight to the sofa now. All my efforts are wasted. What if I have to do it all over again? Change my name. Move elsewhere. Restart my business and talk to no one, so I won't get attached.

"You didn't fail. It's not your fault and never was," Avel said.

He then placed his hands on mine and softly removed the grip I had on his poor sofa.

"He won't be able to get near you. I can guarantee it," he said, his golden eyes deep in mine.

"How?" I asked, so spellbound, I no longer am afraid.

"Until he's rid of, you'll never be alone," he said, a plan surely simmering in his head.

"Why would you do this for me?"

"It's a selfish deed, really."

That brought me out of the trance and back into confusion. A selfish deed is for one's own good. Why would this be for his...

"I want to keep you safe," he continues. "I've never wanted to see someone smile so much before. I'm not one to say things like these, but I'll regret it if I don't."

Colour me shocked at this ambiguous confession.

"Does this mean what I think it means?" I ask to make sure.

His hands were already on mine, but he now held them dearly.

"It's whatever you want to think it is."

I yield to my human impulses and surrender control. I chose to free fall on him and embrace his frame.

"Can I?" I ask, trusting he knows what I mean.

He responds to my touch with his own and holds my waist. Closing my eyes, I bring my lips to tenderly rest on his. I sink into slow motion when our lips perfectly fuse. I find solace in the affectionate kiss, as if it's a refuge from the chaos of my world.

Chapter 28

I ease my body away from him, but stay close. My hands fall back to my sides until Avel takes hold of them. His eyes have become so much more honest. They're raw. Just like gold in its original form. The kiss we shared had passion, yet it burned thinly and gradually, easing us into this tranquil state. I couldn't have been more composed and more in love. That kiss was the answer to questions we never asked.

"I have to tell you something," he says, holding my hands tighter. "I can only say that to you." His voice dropped an octave.

"Go ahead."

"Things might change if I tell you, but it's not something I want to hide from the one I love."

My heart.

He breathed deeply, bracing himself for what was to come.

"I'm the Crystal Mask," he announced, his pupils shaking.

"Come again?"

"I'm the Crystal Mask," he repeats, enunciating every syllable.

Colour me thunderstruck. Sitting as still as a statue, not a single muscle twitches or eyelash bats. My mind stopped running.

I've never even suspected anyone near me to be the Crystal Mask.

Avel?

The Crystal Mask?

The blue-eyed man who smelled like musk?

The man in front of me has golden amber eyes and smells like a fragrant soap. Out of nowhere, a wave of embarrassment hits me. I want to disappear, to become invisible. I realize I had interacted with him before, oblivious to his identity. When thinking the Crystal Mask was another person, I nearly fell into his mysterious spell but then fell for Avel's. Since they're one person, that means I fell twice.

Covering my face with my hands, I inevitably bring Avel's too.

"What's wrong?" he asked, glancing around.

My face has, without a doubt, turned red.

"Don't look at me."

"Why shouldn't I?" he says, trying to take down our hands, but I pull them back.

"You go beyond my expectations. Is this how you express anger?"

"You've seen my anger the first time we met. You should know this isn't it."

"Then what is it?" he asks, a chuckle in his words.

"I'm thinking of the day you came to my place in disguise and how I talked to you..."

"And how did you talk to me? It was a bit weird, I admit. Normally, you should have been hysterical. You should have screamed and hit me with pillows or, better, a pan."

With that, I loosened up and dropped our hands.

"I wanted to watch you longer," I say, keeping my eyes on his, the image of the Crystal Mask's overlapping.

Everything's been said and I can be more honest with myself. I can admit my feelings for Avel that I thought were taboo. That's what love was to me. It was naïve of me to judge a concept I hadn't properly experienced.

Now I can get as close as I want to Avel. I can kiss him and wrap my arms around him anytime I desire to. The desire to be as close as possible to him overcomes me. With a cramped sofa, the difficulty level to that is quite low. Within a second, my body already lies on his and my hands rest on his chest. Automatically, he embraces me with his arms and gently rests his chin on my head. There's nothing to fear in his arms. His embrace has become my secret garden.

"So you're the Crystal Mask, huh?" I whisper, burrowed in him.

"You're not shocked?"

"Of course I am. It's just that my feelings aren't changing because of the news."

My emotions are in turmoil. While I was captivated by the Crystal Mask, and rooting for his mission, I never agreed to his ways. Now, I think it must have been suffocating for Avel when he realized this was the only way to fulfil his mission. I give him a firm hug to acknowledge his hardships. His life's been a gamble since the day he'd chosen to take action. All that's left to wonder was why he'd made that choice in the first place.

And so I asked him, "Why did you feel it was you who had to wear the mask?"

He closed his eyes and took in a deep inhale.

"Never once did I feel I had to wear the mask. I'm not special, nor am I not the chosen one. I was just tired. I wanted to clean this town and live in a corruption-free space. My ways may be old fashion or simply wrong, but forgive me for my head could only come up with this solution."

He held me up and made it so we could see eye to eye. Then he looked at me, his eyes flickering with innocence. Who knew I'd ever think Avel was child-like? His glass mask is full of cracks, yet every piece is spotless.

"It's your dream, isn't it? To live where corruption's a myth. I'll help you," I said.

Instincts took over me as I suddenly want to clear the entire world for him. I want to replace the stormy clouds in his sky with eternal sunshine.

"I don't want your help. It's not to drag you into my mess that I confessed my identity. It's because I don't want to tell lies in your company. I wanted to show you my everything. The thought of having you involved never crossed my mind, and it never will."

"But I agree with you."

"Not with my method, I can tell. Keeping my secret is how you can help.

Feign ignorance towards it. Then again, I wouldn't blame you if you reported me. I suppose this means I ask nothing of you."

"You're being stubborn. I can't win with you."

"No, you can't," he says, a triumphant smile to him. "Let's go back to the subject of you."

"What's there to say add? I told you the gist."

"I'll do the talking this time. I'm worried about you. That Claud is roaming the town I've been trying so hard to protect from harm. The harm is making its way directly to you and I want to protect you like I want to protect Mardi Town. You're part of it, if not bigger to me. I can't let a thing happen to you. You'll stay with me, in my office, in my home. In times we can't be together, you'll be with Ace or Robert at Java Haze. I don't want you on your own for even a second. You can take care of yourself, I know. But I also know that Claud triggers you. Freezes you. Changes you. Until we can get him to leave town, promise me you'll do as I say."

He leaned in his pinkie ever so cutely, waiting for me to cross it. Tears in my eyes as I weave our fingers together. No one's ever been as caring and as determined to keep me safe.

It's almost funny how quickly our relationship evolved. Rather than saying it has evolved, we could say it was well hidden and only now can the colours show.

After making the promise, we walked to my apartment as I organized a few necessities in a suitcase. When Avel said I'd needed to be with him, he meant it. He wants me to live in his house for the time being, considering Claud has my address and the means to stalk me—if he wished to. It's challenging to pack when I don't know how long I'll be away for. In case of need, I can always return here with Avel or a trusted person.

How ever could we convince Claud to leave? What if he decides to settle here and pretend to have given up for me to be at ease again and walk alone so he'd confront me again? What if he's that persistent? The thought of it makes my heart race with fear. I'll admit that Avel can be quite scary when he wants to, but will it be enough? A person as stupid as Claud won't be scared so easily. He lacks common sense and sense in general. It's as if Avel picks up on my angst because every now and then, he pats my head or my back or my shoulders, or my hands. His touch is soothing and emits warmth that is shared throughout my entire body.

I love this affectionate version of Avel. It shocks me every time, but I'm never repulsed. He feels like a completely different person while still maintaining the Avel essence. The Avel essence is somewhat of a cool mint infused with Irish whisky. His affectionate side brings some maple syrup to the mix.

After I'd packed my suitcase and brought it to my new resting place, Avel walked me to Java Haze. It'd be hard to stay in his office today, since his schedule is packed with meetings. When I told him I didn't mind waiting in an empty office, he shared with me his paranoid worries. He says I'd be out of his sight and that Claud could find me anywhere. Personally, I'd doubt he'd look for me at the bank, let alone receive permission to enter an office. I complied for Avel to be at ease.

"Call me if anything happens. There's a lot I can do from afar," he said, his hand holding mine tight.

"Focus on your meetings."

"They're insignificant when they're led by Louella, who is corruption at its best."

"I've always been curious about what Louella's done. It says it on her face that she's done something, but what?"

"Now, now, I can't reveal sensitive information on a busy street. Your curiosity will have to wait, my love."

That is when my heart decided to pause.

My love. My love. My love.

The whisky is giving me a sugar rush. I think he poured too much maple syrup. I take it back. There can never be too much.

Chapter 29

I'd been at Java Haze for a few hours before I received a call from Ace. He called to say he had news regarding my messed up apartment. Of course, he was informed of my promise with Avel and came directly to Java Haze to bring me to the station. I'll admit, that's embarrassing. He's busy, he has a job, he's a police officer, yet he came to escort me. It's close by, so it must not have been a big deal, but my thoughts exactly. I could've made a run for it and get to the station in no time. Even if I do encounter Claud, what's he gonna do in a busy street? Bite me?

"You don't have to look away. It's nothing, really," Ace said, noticing my grimace.

"It's nothing for me too," I say, unable to meet his eyes.

The escort's not the only matter that preoccupies me. I was more friendly with Ace than with Avel. Now it's the opposite. Does that change things with Ace? I overthink when aware of the fact Ace knows too—that the dynamics of Avel and I's relationship did a full 180. In reality, my behaviour doesn't need to change when with Ace. I'm dating Avel, not the both of them. He's my friend, at least I hope so.

"Tell me, Ace, do you consider me as a friend?" I carefully ask, fully knowing it's out of character for me to say something this soft.

"They claim people change when falling in love and I can see it's right," he says, a grin on his face. "We've been friends for a while now. From the time I saw you in the club, I thought we'd be great friends. Did you not consider me as a friend?"

"I did. I did. I was just unsure if you did, too. We've never acknowledged it."

"It's true that if you never put it into words, one may never know for sure," he said, wiser than I could ever be.

I've lost two friends, and not too long after, gained two new friends—I consider Avel to be my friend just as much as he is my lover.

They didn't replace them. It's purely coincidental that they match in number. Given that life isn't always fair, it wouldn't be logical to lose something and receive a copy of it in return for me to call it fair. It didn't take their loss for me to find Avel and Ace. I could have had four amazing friends, or I could have lost Auburn and Laine and never met Avel and Ace. In whatever way it happened, I'd still consider it unfair, since perfection is unachievable. Instead, I found bliss I can subjectively call perfection.

At the station, Ace brought me to a private conference room. I sat down while he stood near the board. Turning on the projector, he started the briefing. I feel like I'm an executive in a police TV show waiting for someone to show me a worthy lead on the investigation closely watched by the media.

"After a bit of research, I found that there is another person in town with a business of the same type as yours. Of course, that alone is not enough to suspect them."

The board showed a bright mint green logo that said, P.O. Temp. Rentals.

"With a bit of digging, mostly through their activities and revenues, I noticed something that's suspicious."

The slide changed to a graph showing the revenue of the said company.

"As you can see, during the time you started your business, P.O. Temp. Rentals had started to observe a downfall, and it only started to fall when your business grew. Your companies climbed a see-saw. As one went up, the other went down. And that's life. If a business offers better service, people are sure to choose it. While it indicates they hold a motive, it doesn't prove a single thing yet. Onto the next slide."

The next slide shows yet another graph of revenues, but it looks different. The numbers seem to be better.

"As you can see, right after your incident, their revenues experienced growth. They're not back to their original numbers, but if your location is out of business for longer, they'll fully return."

"It's a suspicion and a lead, too?" I ask, crossing my legs.

"Yes, and that's the only thing I can provide you. I lack the authority to investigate further in the absence of concrete proof. As an ally, though, I can at least tell you his name because you have another ally that is particularly knowledgeable when it comes to rich people's houses."

So he knows and might've been the one aiding the Crystal Mask all this time.

"That's more than enough. Thank you. But can I ask you a question?"

"Shoot."

"Since when did you know Avel?"

I'm wondering how they came to be. Were they friends before the start of the Crystal Mask? Or did they meet to join force on their common goal? I mean, Ace is also a fan of having a double identity.

"I don't remember when exactly we first met, but we shared similar ideas. The idea didn't occur to us immediately. What we shared was hatred towards the world. We bonded on that. We both wanted to be protectors, but chose different paths for it."

Believe it or not, this clears up a lot. It all makes sense, and I am more than satisfied with the answer. It's lacking detail, but that just makes it the more interesting. There is an abundance of things for me to uncover about these two.

On a piece of paper, Ace wrote for me the name Gabriel Hill. It rang no bell. I've never heard of this person or even of his business. It surprises me that it took me, a single business, to shake his down. Must not have been a good one to begin with.

I'm reluctant to send his name to Avel, because I know he'll inquire about it or even investigate by himself. I don't have to tell him it's about an enemy, but it won't take him long to guess. If I can find this Gabriel Hill without the Crystal Mask's help, then I'd be okay. Even then, the situation's tough since Avel doesn't let me be on my own. I can't bring Ace, for fear I jeopardize his job. Giving me that information was dangerous enough.

The only place I can meet the man without Avel is Java Haze. There we have Robert. I can't let him on this sensitive information. I'll accuse the man of illegally interfering with my business and he'll either be highly offended if I'm wrong or he'll threaten me further if I'm right.

The lead seems increasingly accurate the more I consider it. My apartment was strategically ruined so that I'd need to replace all furniture and spend a fortune on cleaning. They're all business expenses I'll never get back, unless I find an innovative way to double my profits. This act was without a doubt a shady business decision. Who other than my only concurrence? Hotels are also concurrence, but would those large enterprises deem it necessary to resort to lowly methods for a pawn like me?

Ultimately, I must meet this man. I'll risk it then and I'll risk it now by sending his name to Avel. I'll take the chance, prepared for the barrage of questions I won't be able to answer. I'll even brave Claud and return to Java Haze alone. Ace is busy. Let's not interrupt him any further.

This is ridiculous. Of course I can walk by myself. The freezing on the spot was a one-time thing. I'll show Claud that Audra Frye is gone. I regret breaking the promise so early on, but a little walk won't do harm and he'll never have to know. Ace is on it.

"I can count on you, Ace? It's better for you, too. Avel won't enjoy hearing you didn't walk me back."

"Even more so the reason I need to walk you back," he said in a frown.

"Trust me on this one. Be my

accomplice apart from Avel, for once."

In mere seconds, I'd won.

349

Chapter 30

"I can find out what this is about without you telling me. You know that," Avel said to me on the phone.

From Java Haze, I sent him a message in hopes I could resolve this before he knew anything of it. He'll find out for sure. But he'll have nothing to do if I fixed the matter myself. If he doesn't want to involve me in his matters, I hope he understands I hold the same will for mine.

"Please give me the address. I won't do anything rash. I won't go there."

"That's a promise?"

"Do you always need the word promise

to confirm everything?"

"Yes," he says, his voice solemn.

Something tickles my brain every time he uses the word promise. It's as though he used the word out of fear. Now I'm the one who wants to protect him and his fragile heart.

"I promise," I said, knowing I'll rue these words.

"I can't deny it now," he says, with a sigh. "I'll send you the address as soon as I can, but I'm watching you. Literately. I'm coming over to the café soon. If I don't find you there, I'm calling a missing person search."

"I didn't know you were so talkative and so threatening. You missed your vocation."

He let out a small chuckle; "and what job would have been right for me?"

"Um... A prosecutor."

"Never in hell would I become a prosecutor."

"I'm only saying that, given your personality, you would have made a hell of a good prosecutor."

In reality, I'm glad he chose the banker path. We wouldn't have met if he'd chose otherwise. Sure, our first meeting was the worst I'd had with a new person, but it took a turn and we landed in a relationship full of sparks. We would've still met as robber and victim, but it'll lead us nowhere since I never got to see the Crystal Mask after.

"I'll see you soon," he said, ending the call.

Butterflies swarmed in my belly at the idea of him by my side again.

***

It took five minutes for the Crystal Mask to send me my desired information. Impressing, isn't it? There's no time to be impressed.

I borrowed a sheet of paper and an envelope from Robert. We're going at it old fashion. I can't directly go to his house and I don't have a phone number. My best bet is to write him a letter to then arrange a meeting. I won't hint in the letter that I suspect him. I'll pretend to be a customer and write that I'm bad with technology and would prefer to receive answers to my questions face to face. My brain has these genius moments every so often.

I quickly finished the letter and hid it in my bag. I'll have to wait for the right moment to send it without getting caught. The first promise we made now seems harder to keep. What even is this situation? I'm not allowed to go anywhere by myself and the only people I trust are tattle tales that tell Avel my every move. This is already getting stifling. To grasp that I'll live like this until Claud gives up drives me mad.

Is there not a period of grace where you can change your mind on a promise? Just like the five-second-rule that suggests you can eat food dropped on the floor if it hasn't been there for more than five seconds.

We've only started to open up and I

don't want to go back on something he finds so important. Who knows what it'll trigger in him? I suppose I can at least discuss it with him. I can bargain my way to easing the restrictions. Or show him the promise is useless since my behaviour in front of Claud was a fluke.

Just as I am thinking of him, I capture him out the window, walking to the cafe in his long coat. We matched eyes for a second there and that smile he gave me brought electricity to run through me. The gold in his eyes are conductors.

"I see you're listening," he said, taking a seat next to me.

I show a smile in response, but it was forced. How do I even go about this?

"About that," I say.

"Something wrong?"

"Yeah, I guess I was a bit too quick to make that promise."

"You can talk to me about it," he said, his fingers softly caressing my hand.

"I don't feel suffocated yet, but I anticipate I will. I like my freedom and being unable to roam alone robs me of it. It turns me weak. I'm touched by how much you would do to protect me, but I don't want to be dependant."

I eyed Avel, worried. Worried of his reaction and if I'd hurt him by refusing the hand he doesn't easily reach out to anyone. The thought of how it must feel makes me ache on his behalf.

Avel left the weight of his hand on mine and ceased the caress. There was no noticeable shift in his expression, as if he was a master at hiding his true feelings.

"I understand. I never wanted to control your life. As my feelings for you intensified, I reckon I grew rash and, without thinking deeply enough, imposed on you impossible things. It was all with good intentions but clearly lacking in consideration. Just understand that my concerns are real and I'm at a point where I could do anything to keep you safe. You're more of a priority to me than any of my endeavours. It's the first time I felt this way and I'm in a maze. There's no logical reason for me to suddenly act this way, but here I am. Weird, isn't it?"

All I want to do is take him in my arms. How sweet and endearing of him. Despite the unfamiliarity of his words, I still recognize the same person I'd met at the bank.

Day by day, I like him more and notice those feelings formed a while ago. I'll allow myself to love. To rid myself of prejudices I have about love. Funny how a good man is all it took. Though when you think about it, a bad man was all it took to close my doors, therefore this makes sense.

"Avel," I tell him, as I hold off from putting my hand to his cheek—because I'd be mortified with embarrassment if Robert caught us. "Thank you."

Two simple words meant the end of an eternity of sufferance and he knows it. I trust he now knows how grateful I am for his attention and care. With an ease of restrictions and the resolution of problems, we'll get along just fine.

Hand in hand, we walked out of the

café. I never suspected Avel would be the affectionate type, yet he was the one to ask for my hand. With every step, my reality turned brighter as he smiled over and over again.

"Avel, I just have to ask you something."

"Anything."

"Were you always this happy-go-lucky or was I blind this entire month?"

"You weren't blind," he laughed, the corner of his eyes crinkling. "I was holding off. You see, I was intrigued by you for far longer than you'd expect. I saw you at Java Haze before I saw you at the bank."

"You did? How come I never saw you?"

"Because you were always so focused on your work that you had eyes for none. That made you even more fascinating to me."

"That's stalking behaviour we're talking about then," I tease.

"Is catching a few glances here and there a crime?"

"If it doesn't go further, I guess not."

"Let me continue then," he said, tugging at my hand. "When we started interacting,

I was scared of how well we bonded and thought it'd be dangerous to take it further given that I'm the Crystal Mask. So I ignored my feelings and tried to avoid you. Later, I had a glimmer of hope when you talked positively about my other persona. Of course, I don't want you to praise my methods or encourage me in any way. I'm a criminal and there's no way I'll let you agree with me."

"I agree with your intentions," I cut him off. "But I don't think you should burden yourself with fixing this broken society."

What pushed him to this point? Everyone longs for peace, but few act on the desire. It's not because they lack the courage. It's because life won't be fair to them once they try. Avel is bound to face consequences if discovered. The thought of it is so terrifying that I can't even bring myself to imagine it.

"I didn't think so either," he said, an air of melancholy in his tone. "But I had little to lose. Now that I do, it's conflicting."

I halt in my tracks and pull him closer.

"Are you considering ending the Crystal Mask?" I asked, my eyes wide.

His lips became a crescent moon. "Maybe I am. I can be content with the idea of spending my days with you. Even in a soiled society, I'd be happy. But it'd be a little selfish."

"Not at all," I assure him, wrapping my arms around him. "That would only be fair to you. You deserve inner peace and love."

His eyes beamed with mellowness as he asked, "could I really have it all?"

Yes. Yes. Yes.

Rising on the tip of my toes, I placed a soft kiss on his cheek. I want to bring back colours in this man's world.

"It's all going to be okay now," I say.

"I trust you," he said in return before he set his hands on my cheeks to then press his lips against mine.

Chapter 31

A week. I spent a week already in Avel's home. It's been nothing but sweet. He let me have the guest room, as he planned when we'd first made the crazy promise. He lifted the restrictions, but I stayed here by choice. My belongings were already here, thus I saw no wrong with it. He took two days off and stayed home with me. For the most part, we talked and learned more about one another. I took in his perspective of life and him, mine. To share insightful conversations day and night was bliss for the mind.

On the days when he had to clock in at

the bank, I killed time at home with admin tasks and the binge reading of books. I turned into something I never expected to become; a homebody. That life doesn't seem too bad either. Needless to say, I wouldn't have enjoyed it as much without the assurance of Avel's return by the end of the day. What are measly hours when you know you'll spend the rest of them with the one you love?

We played cards and shared espressos. We even cooked a few times and Avel admitted to having never used his kitchen before. His fridge was filled with takeout containers and water bottles. He told me things would be different now that he had someone to care for. Then I told him this was not a good excuse. That it shouldn't have taken the start of a relationship for him to start up-keeping more than the basic needs. You could say I pushed him towards a path of self-love. It's the most important kind of love. I'd loved myself so well I could teach another and fully embrace his presence. Days with Avel were well spent and filled with liveliness.

How did I live without this man by my side? Don't get me wrong, I'm perfectly capable of living on my own and feel complete. My work was fulfilling enough. Avel is simply the unexpected addition I wasn't aware I needed. What's more than completion? Infinity. When I'm with Avel, life feels limitless. I'm full on my own, but I radiate his light.

"I hate Mondays," he told me while arranging his vest in front of the mirror.

"You chose to work at a bank. No one forced you."

"That's the destiny of a guy with no dreams."

"It's never too late," I say, my eyes following his movements.

"I'll need your help if I suddenly find myself a dream, though."

"Not a problem. Wake me at four because of an epiphany and I'll still help you."

With each step towards me on the sofa, his beaming smile grew brighter and more contagious.

"I'll see you after work. Do you want to meet at Java Haze today?"

"You're allowing me to walk alone, or are you gonna bother Ace again?" I say, pressing my chin down.

"You don't have to worry today. I can guarantee you the streets are safe."

He peered at me with unwavering eye contact.

"What did you do?"

"I haven't done anything yet, but Claud's waiting for me at the station. He's currently held for stalking charges, but I'll make sure he leaves town before the sun goes down."

"I don't care for his well being, but please don't use violence."

"We'll just talk. You'll be surprised by how much you can achieve with words alone," he says, stealing a kiss.

I'm worried his words won't go through since Claud is dumb enough to mistake anger for jealousy. I wouldn't be shocked if he believes Avel perceives him as a rival and that I still haven't moved on. That I mention his name on every occasion, infuriating the heck out of Avel.

"I'll walk you to Java Haze, if you'd like to go now."

I take him up on the offer and throw on the first sweater I see laying on top of my suitcase.

***

"Can you explain to me why a letter for you was sent to my coffee shop? Do you not have an address?" Robert asked me, holding an envelope with the name Gabriel Hill printed at the front.

"Sorry..." I tell him, receiving the letter with two hands. "It won't happen again. I really had no choice. Do me a favour and keep it a secret from Avel or whoever asks."

"Who's this Gabriel Hill? Are you cheating already with Avel?" he says, completely ignoring my request.

"What do you mean, already? Did you

expect me to cheat during this relationship?"

I'm able to joke around while I fiddle trying to open this damn letter.

Robert cackled and nearly lost his balance. "Sorry. I mis-phrased. Even if it was a joke, I admit I said it badly."

I'm more fortunate than I thought. See, this man is precious. That's it. I'm officially taking him as my father. I'll never tell him because he'll be embarrassed and avoid me like the plague for the next month or so. No, I'll let him know with subtle actions.

In parallel, I'll learn how to maintain a healthy father-daughter relationship by being an outstanding daughter. It'll take some learning, but I'm all for it. I'll take him out for coffee—though he'll criticize their method of brewing with scrutiny. I'll take him camping—and convince him to leave that coffee shop for the weekend. We'll have the time of our lives. Slight changes can indeed bring major results.

As I eventually get the letter out of the envelope, my eyes grow wide, reading its content. Who schedules a meeting on the day of when sending a letter? What if I hadn't been here today and picked up the mail days later?

It seems I won't need to break the second promise we made after all, but instead go around it. I am meeting the man, but not at his address. No, he proposed we talk in a park not far from here. While it is unconventional, I find it'd make it easier for me to return to Java Haze before Avel has the chance to notice I was gone.

"Thank you for the coffee, Robert. I'll be back soon. I have things to fix," I say, gathering my belongings.

Robert put a hand on the strap of my bag before I could grab it. "I don't know what this letter was or where you're going, but promise me you'll be careful."

The men in my life and their promises...

"I pinky promise," I say, extending a pinky.

He doesn't extend his and sends a nod my way in exchange. I like that he doesn't change; it's reassuring.

***

I sat on a bench in the park, the hands in my pocket shaking. I'm starting to understand Avel's reasoning with those promises. Forget about Claud, I could potentially be meeting a very dangerous man, that without a weapon or an emergency exit. Then again, we're in a park. Who would dare to attempt crime in broad daylight here?

With my boots, I kick the snow underneath my feet to keep warm. Spring doesn't seem any closer. It's as though the cold gained authority to deny its entry. Open the doors, I beg you. I'm freezing.

Just then, a man started approaching me. He's dressed in all black, from head to toe, to his sun glasses... Oh no.

"I guessed it'd be you, Rene. Even the elderly of Mardi Town would have opted for a phone call at the least."

"Mr. Pacheco? You're Gabriel Hill?" I say, my loud voice echoing throughout the empty park.

He avoided my gaze and took a seat next to me.

"I may be."

I can't believe my eyes or my ears; or my brain for allowing his words to come through.

"And are you the one who ravaged my apartment?" I ask, holding my breath.

"Mardi Town didn't need your business. We were doing just fine," he says, his breathing noisy.

This can't be real. He's the man I idolized. The one I'd wished to be taught by. How does anyone expect me to process this? Why does life keep shattering my expectations? From friendships to a potential mentor... Maybe the fault lies in myself. From the start, I was in the wrong for expecting. Not for the reason that I think I can only attract negativity, but just as you wouldn't put your own expectations on your child, you wouldn't put them on your creation. Life is just that, your creation. A reflection of your thoughts. The key might be to surrender to these thoughts and let life unfold the way it's meant to.

"I'll report you to the police," I say, my survival instincts at last kicking in.

"You won't be able to," he says, confidence in his voice.

"Who are you to decide?"

"I'm no one to decide what you choose, but I can influence you. You see, I know a few things that could put that boy of yours in peril."

My heart dropped. I don't even want to hear it. I'm not dumb enough to let the words between his lines go over my head. I'm well aware of what his message entails. Aware, but I remain bewildered. The conflicts this man is giving me are enough for me to want to blame all my past problems on him. It'll bring me comfort to have a singular source to blame when I recall the difficult times. 'Ah, Mr. Pacheco is to blame for the family I was born into.

I'll curse him to death. Ah, Mr. Pacheco put a bug in Auburn's mind and she betrayed my trust. Screw him. I'm happy now with Avel by my side.' He's deserving of hatred he didn't cause.

"Speak. Tell me what you want," I tell him, not wasting time.

Truly, I want this to be over. I want to live a life where Avel is on the right path and I follow close by.

Mr. Pacheco takes off his sunglasses and I bear witness to the eyes he's hidden for so long. I guess being mysterious doesn't always lead to drop-dead-gorgeous. The bags under his eyes take up most of the space and are of a purple shade I could never achieve, no matter how many sleepless nights I spend.

"I can give you a chance. If you quit this business of yours, I'll leave your boy alone. He'll stay by your side and everyone's gonna be happy."

What is it I wouldn't do to protect him? When I said I wanted to bring him eternal sunshine, I meant it. I might've used many metaphors, but I never took them lightly. The moment Mr. Pacheco gave me the ultimatum, my mind was made. The choice isn't weak or pathetic. I'm not giving my life away for a man. I'm letting myself know of the priorities I hold. Even that career of mine, it never was my dream. What good is money for if you're basking in it alone? I'll take this opportunity to find a career that brings me both money and ambition. I'll be Avel's emotional support just as much as he'll be mine. Avel is ready for a change. He's willing to better himself and his life. Who would I be if I let this despicable man trample over his courage?

"Do you really promise you'll keep quiet if I do as you say?"

"I'm a businessman. I don't make promises I can't keep," he says, reaching a hand out.

Does that apply to shady business men?

Still, I take a leap and shake his hand.

"One more thing," he says, his hand still gripping mine, the touch dry and crinkled.

Every second of his grip is torture.

"Tell your boy to not target me."

"You won't have to worry about it. He's planning on retiring, you see."

"Very good choice," he says, the corners of his lips reaching high.

He keeps shaking my hand and I fear I'll see his grin in my nightmares.

Chapter 32

Avel's point of view

Finally, I have him in front of me. The plague that robbed Rene of her freedom. He grins at my sight, and I can't help but think something's wrong with his head. Isn't there?

"You're here to give her up?" he says, the wind doing me a favour by obstructing my view of his face with strands of his hair.

Ace was nice enough to accord me five minutes with Claud at the back of the station. That only after I assured him my fists wouldn't leave my pockets.

I won't entertain the plague for too long.

"I'm here to tell you to leave town," I say, a fist forming in the pocket of my coat.

I'm trying to stay calm and to resolve this matter without delay.

"Who are you to Rene?" he then asks, putting all of his strength in his eyes.

"I'm hers."

His face turned red and his stance tightened.

"She's a man-eater. You don't know how many men she had in her hometown. That's the reason I broke up with her." He ran his mouth with words that couldn't be more deceitful.

If I ripped his head apart, would Rene still love me? She might have tolerated theft, but murder would be crossing the line.

"I'll gladly let her eat me then," I say, my fist loosening.

This guy's not worth wrath. That would

be needless attention.

Now, how to get rid of him?

"You're just saying this to act cool, but really, do you think you can handle her?"

This guy makes me laugh; now I've had my dose. Time's not meant to be wasted on people that disgrace the human race. The problem with those people is that they're absurdly persistent in a losing game. They lose sight of morals and chase their goal with a tunnel vision. Don't mistake his actions for an inspirational mindset, he's a pest, and that's all he is.

"If you don't get out of town, I'll ruin the entire life you built within the day," I say calmly, giving him the chance of a lifetime.

Were he to refuse, the next words won't be as docile. I'll surrender my need for retribution, since I'll never be fully satisfied. Ruining his life won't nearly be enough to appease me. Were he to die, I'd think he'd had it too easy. Without the knowledge of what lies after death, I'll assume the pain he'd inflicted outweighs the pain of dying by a considerable margin. I'll imagine he's resting in peace, away from the pressure of life. What I want for him is to suffer endlessly. Death is unable to realize my wish. I hope he understands the favour I'm doing him.

"Who are you to chase me out? You have no authority. And how are you going to ruin my life? What do you know about my life?"

Wrong move, pest.

"If I'd wanted, I could learn of the exact day you took your first step and determine the day you'll take your last."

You get the message now, pest?

"You think you're god or what?" he mutters under his breath.

His figure grew smaller and those eyes he gave so much strength to, eased their way out of my sight and onto the nearest tree.

I want to break his tunnel, forcing him to go past it.

"What do you say?" I ask him. "Leave and I'll spare you. You have no purpose here. Rene's moved on and so should you. This persistency of yours will bring you to dead end after dead end. Why waste your time?"

It pained me to be this nice and offer him valuable advice. Alas, it's more effective to think you're engaging with a five-year-old for your words to reach a person of a similar mental age.

He scrunched his face and I think he understands all I'd said was right. He too appears conscious there was no chance of putting back Rene in his net to begin with. Even without me, her protector, she somehow would have kicked him to the curb. Rene's a capable woman. She's an inspiration. I have much to learn from how she loves and lives.

"I didn't exactly come here hoping I'd get back with her," he says in a poor attempt to keep face. "I was just visiting, because it's been a while. Even if I wasn't able to see her for long, I can still say I fulfilled the purpose of my visit. So I guess I'll go."

He muttered that last part in a near whisper as he shifted his gaze around, blinking rapidly.

My anger is only subduing when I try to ignore the mental images Rene's brief description of her past conceived. And as I watch him go past the gate, I attempt to erase them whole. I'll let bygones be bygones since I can't change the past. Instead, I'll go above and beyond to ensure Rene's present and future are filled with smiles, laughs, and butterflies.

I return to the station, where I spot Ace pacing around the place. The minute I step into his range of view, he comes rushing. He rests his hands on my shoulders and stares at me, his brows tense.

"Avel, I don't want to lose Rene's trust, but I don't want her in danger either. Through my own research, I discovered the true identity of that Gabriel Hill. He's a dangerous man who stands to nothing to monopolize his sectors. More importantly, that man is Mr. Pacheco."

"Why is Rene in danger?" I shout,

regardless of the fact that I am in a police station.

"He's the one that damaged her apartment and I gave her his name and you, his address." Ace's face paled when realization hit him.

Not needing to ask more, I stormed out of the station.

Please let Rene be sitting at Java Haze unharmed inside and out.

It takes me no time to reach the shop and can breathe easy when I see her sitting at the counter, snacking on... bread sticks?

"Are you okay?" I ask instinctively as I hold her cheeks.

"I'm perfectly fine," she says, her lips curving. She gave the kind of smile one would have after the ending of a long story where one is content with its resolution.

That expression worries me. Something had to happen. I have no doubts.

"Robert added bread sticks to the menu. Isn't that great?"

I don't expect her to be honest, but I'd love it if she were. I'm sure she's really not that interested in bread sticks.

"I know about Gabriel Hill, or should I say, Mr. Pacheco?" I blurt out.

"Oh, so you know," she says, bringing a stick to her mouth, seemingly unfazed by my confession.

Did I by accident say 'I know about tomorrow's weather' instead?

"Don't go find him. He's–" I was about to warn when she beat me to the truth.

"The person who threatened my business? You don't have to worry. It's all fixed. No harm will come to the both of us."

"What do you meant the both of us?"

She broke character for a second there when staying silent a bit too long.

"Nothing. I meant nothing. I misspoke. I meant to say he won't harm me or my business anymore. Yes. That's the two I mentioned."

The rushed babbling makes it obvious she's hiding something. I believe in Rene and her ability to resolve problems, but I'm afraid of the sacrifices she'd had to make.

I don't dig further, bearing in mind I'll merely stress her out. Rene's stubborn; she won't accept the help easily. She'll be devoted to keep her sacrifice under the covers.

I need to see that man. I need to go there prepared. The Crystal Mask has one last mission before retirement, it appears. One worth the ending of a glorious story.

Chapter 33

Rene's point of view

He's suspicious of me. I can tell by the way he switched the subject to bread sticks that day. He knew I'd met with Mr. Pacheco and didn't say a thing. I thought he'd freak out, or at least ask me about the promise–it meant so much to him. Then I could assure him I technically did not break it. He was the one to tell me the streets were safe.

He acted like we were a new couple eating bread sticks at our regular café because problems were a thing of the past. And they are. I'd be happy if Avel swiped the whole show under the rug. Except I know Avel could never. He's suppressing. He's letting ideas simmer in his brain.

Now it's me that can't keep my eyes off him. I'd love to keep him with me at all times and make sure he's nowhere near Mr. Pacheco. Worry starts to invade my space when I realize that's exactly what he could be doing. We're not in the same room since today I had to visit a few landlords to report that I'll be breaking my lease shortly.

I called Avel with no success. Next, I sent countless of messages to warn him against whatever he had in mind. He doesn't need to share for me to know. I've been careless and foolish for giving him the time and opportunity to walk right into the lion's den.

In the streets, I sprint without the knowledge of where exactly they'd meet. I hoped to cross their paths by chance. If luck could be on my side this one time, I'll ask nothing of it again. I run and I run, fearing the worst.

At last, I think of the park. If Avel reached out first, it's possible Mr. Pacheco chose the location—as he did with me. Nearing the park, I hold the fantasy that Avel isn't this reckless and I find him walking out of the bank for his 2pm coffee break.

Dreams don't all come true. Avel and Mr. Pacheco stand in the middle of the park, the space for a car between them.

I sprint to Avel and tug on the sleeves of his coat. What can I do to stop this man?

"Don't, Avel. He knows you're the Crystal Mask and can expose you any time he wants," I remind him in case the dozen of messages went through an eye and out the other.

"Don't worry, my love. I've come prepared," he said, extending me a wink.

This doesn't reassure me at all. In fact, it pushes me further into my sea of worries.

"Listen well, Andrea, Leonardo, Giovanni, Tommaso, Nicola, Raffaele, Vito,

Pacheco," Avel starts to say, stunning both Mr. Pacheco and I.

"How are you familiar with my entire name?" he says, his tone quieter.

"I know everything about you," Avel replies, his words sending chills down my spine.

"Well, I am aware of your nighttime activities. I've already informed your girl about it. Seems the message wasn't clear enough," he says, hands reaching in his pocket. "I can call the police right this moment," he adds, taking his phone out.

"What if I tell you that you'll soon be incapablc of it? I, too, am aware of what you've been up to," Avel says, aggravating the situation.

I tug a few more times at his coat and each time, he shakes his head while giving me soft eyes. Maybe I can trust that Avel can emerge victorious in this battle.

"Nothing you can say will stop me," the man says with a scoff.

"Eat my hat, Andrea," Avel responded with, before marching to Mr. Pacheco's side.

Avel's eyes stared into mine while he hid his mouth with a hand and brought it millimetres away from Mr. Pacheco's ear. I watch as our villain takes off his sunglasses and lets them fall on the snow.

"No!" He shouts once and a few more times. I can't tell where he's peering, but it's certainly not Avel or me. He's off in his own world, seemingly reminiscing about a past far more troubled than mine. That's merely my assumption, though. He took a step back, losing control of his balance. Avel, satisfied by his creation, whistled his way back to my side, his arm now wrapped around my shoulders.

I continued watching Mr. Pacheco, who acted more hysteric by the second. He pulled the little hair he had on his scalp, clung onto a streetlight for support, while sweat dripped from his forehead and his face flushed.

"What did you tell him for him to turn into this?" I ask Avel.

"I just triggered an old and painful

memory. One where the guilt can never cease," he answered, a grin to his words.

"What it is it?" I ask again, curiosity eating me alive.

"You'd rather not know. Let me protect you from this one," he said, rubbing my shoulder.

I'd given up, seeing that the outcome mattered more. Mr. Pacheco looked so out of him. I'm thinking we won't even come across him anywhere in town.

***

Days passed since the incident and indeed, no one had heard of Mr. Pacheco again. Rumour has he was last seen taking a ferry in the middle of the night with a large suitcase. After all the deeds he'd done, it's a shame he gets to leave without facing consequences. And no, it was not the price of Avel's freedom. I'm sure he'll be caught some day for whatever crime he does, because old habits die hard.

Whilst the coast is clear for me to thrive with my business, I'd decided to change paths all the same. I blabbed so much about dreams to everyone without having ever experience one myself. And if not now, when will I ever try? From now on, I won't be reckless with my money. All that for the sake of my unborn dream. Who knows how much I'll need to spend on it because I don't dream small. I'm Rene Mint; passionate and ambitious. That being said, I'll keep my current business alive until I find myself ready to swerve straight into a new venture. What good would it do me to chase a non-existent idea for days on end, and gain nothing out of it?

While Avel buried his crystal mask, Ace announced he'll be pitching a proposal to the force regarding the creation of an anti-corruption division within the police. That division would exclusively work on cleaning the town–much like Avel did in his own ways. Ace mentioned before that Avel and he met with coinciding ideas, but decided on different paths to achieve them. Now, they walk alongside since, as a banker with a substantial amount of insider information, Avel could be an adviser for the division.

Sitting on the sofa in my living room, I tell Avel something I'd always wanted to tell him, "Avel?"

"Yes?" he answered, turning his attention away from the TV to me.

"I love you."

"Took you long enough," he teased.

"Took me long enough? As if you'd said it before me?"

I was deeply offended by something he didn't deserve to say.

"Alright, alright. I'm sorry. I love you more than you can imagine," he said, the gold in his eyes radiating.

His reply was enough to appease all of my day's micro problems and remind me I'll never be alone again. Neither will he.

The End

Acknowledgements

Thank you to my parents for providing me with an environment so peaceful I was able to pour my full energy into this book.

Thank you to the people who've shown interest in my book while I still was in the midst of its creation. I was flattered to know there were people waiting to read it.

Though strange, I'd also like to thank this novel for allowing me to confirm my choice of career. Nearing the end of the book, the work took a toll on me and my mind flooded with doubts. After observing this book from a newly formed perspective, my love for writing returned in the blink of an eye. I even found myself enjoying the dreaded process of editing. And no matter how challenging this book's proven to be, I enjoyed every second of its process.

At long last, I want to thank you, the

person who's read my novel. Words cannot express how grateful I am for the chance you've given to me. I can only say that I'm eternally grateful.

The Mardi Town Series
(All books can be read out of order and
individually)

Deja Vu On Cherry Street (November 18,
2022)

Once In A Glass Wing (May 18, 2023)

The Crystal Mask (April 25, 2024)

More novels coming out in the near
future!

Reviews are of great help to
independent authors.
Consider leaving a review on your
chosen platform, if that's within your
comfort zone.